The Mystery of the

10,000 printed to date—1979
(5-8038—10M—19)
ISBN 0-8474-6300-1

Printed in the United States of America

Contents

Contents

Chapter 1

"Where's Sally?"

Karen Tyler scanned the parking area, looking around at the large group of teens that had met at the church for the annual bike hike. Everyone was talking and laughing as they waited for the signal to leave. There was a bigger group than usual this year because the hike had been combined with the district youth retreat. They were to bike out to the campgrounds, spend the weekend in Bible study and recreation and be back home in time for the Sunday evening service.

Karen looked around again. She didn't see Nita, the German girl who had come to live with them, but she supposed she was around someplace. Karen would have enjoyed the weekend more if Nita had not been invited. But she had been, so there was nothing she could do about it. In fact, Roy had even asked her to give a testimony. Nita didn't seem to know exactly what a testimony was, but she had promised to do it just the same.

Pastor Don, the youth minister, stood on the makeshift platform on the church parking lot and blew a whistle to get everyone's attention, interrupting Karen's thoughts about Nita.

"OK, gang," he shouted. "Let's have prayer, and then before we leave I'd like to give you some last-minute instructions."

A murmur of teen voices filtered across the

parking lot, but everyone quickly quieted down as the pastor began to pray.

"Lord, we want to have a good time this weekend, but we want to learn some real spiritual lessons too," he prayed.

Karen wasn't sure she completely agreed with that. Sure, she was a Christian, but learning lessons made her think of making a commitment of some kind, and that usually meant being restricted in some ways. She wasn't sure she was ready for that. Then, too, she knew her feeling about Nita wasn't right. But it really bothered her when her parents bought clothes and things for Nita and treated her like there was no one else in the house. As a result, Karen found herself feeling extremely jealous of Nita, and try as she would to cover it up, it still showed in almost all of her actions.

As the youth pastor closed his prayer, people started talking again, but Pastor Don quickly blew the shrill-sounding whistle. "We've got only so much time, you know," he said with a smile on his face. "So let's get these announcements over with and be on our way." The group cheered and clapped, then stood quietly beside their bikes to hear the instructions. "Three in a group," shouted the pastor. "You've already been assigned, so get together, travel the route on your instruction sheet, and we'll see you all there—no later than 11 o'clock."

The first group pedaled off, and other groups lined up to be on their way. Karen's group was one of the last to leave. While waiting she looked around to see who Nita was going with. Before she could figure it out, the German girl came over to where she was standing.

"Oh, Karen, this is such fun," she said brokenly. "I am so glad you talked me into going."

"Yeah," Karen said without much enthusiasm. It really hadn't been her idea. Her dad had just announced that he had paid the registration fee for all of them—Karen, Dave and Nita.

"Do you know that I am in the leader's group?" Nita asked excitedly.

"Roy? You're in Roy's group?" The words snapped from Karen's lips in anger.

"Yes, that is his name. Roy. He is in charge of the games and things," Nita replied, not seeming to notice Karen's reaction.

"Who else is in that group?" Karen asked with bitterness.

"Sally Benton," Roy Sparton said, walking over to talk with the two girls.

"Sally?" Karen asked in disbelief. "What is this, a put-up job?"

"Looks like it, doesn't it?" Roy said, laughing. "But you know how we picked the groups—we drew names. I just lucked out, I guess."

"Yeah, lucked out," Karen repeated. "Well, it's almost time for my group to start, so I'll see ya." With that she turned and pushed her bike toward the two teens who were waiting for her.

"Group 11," Pastor Don called, and Karen Tyler was on her way.

"Hey, where's Sally?" Roy called as the next to the last group was leaving.

"I do not know," Nita replied. "I have not seen her at all. Maybe she is not coming."

"Oh, sure she's coming," Roy answered

positively. "She told me she wouldn't miss this retreat for anything."

"Last group," called Pastor Don.

"Sally's not here yet," Roy said. "So I'd like to hold off a few minutes, if that's OK."

"Sure, just don't wait too long," replied the pastor.

"Maybe we should go in the church and call her?" Nita said, making the statement sound like a question.

"Church is locked," the youth pastor said. "I just told the secretary she could leave."

"Don't you have a key?" Roy questioned.

"I left it with my wife in case there was an emergency of some kind."

"Well, you go on," Roy suggested. "Nita and I will wait for a while, and then we'll leave. We'll still get there by 11:00."

The youth pastor took one last glance at the equipment and food in the back of the church van and then took off. He was the only one not going by bike; someone had to get the supplies out to the campgrounds.

"Don't wait too long," he called, swinging around the church parking lot and onto the street.

"Maybe we should go on and just stop by Sally's house," Roy said, still wondering why she hadn't shown up at the church on time. Sally was never late for anything. Something serious had to happen to keep her away from even the regular services. She'd never be late for something special like this. Concern showed on his face.

"Does Sally live around here?" Nita asked, trying to share his concern.

8

"Yeah, we go right by her house," Roy answered. "She lives right on the edge of town."

"Then let us go there; maybe she slept too long or had a flat tire or something."

"Naw, not Sally. If that's what it was, she would have called."

Roy grabbed his bike and kicked back the stand.

"But maybe the church was already locked when she tried," Nita continued, trying to assure Roy that everything was all right.

"I don't think so, Nita. I've got a funny feeling that something's wrong. Come on, let's get going."

Nita mounted her borrowed bike and followed close behind Roy. Sally's house was much closer to the church than Nita had thought. Even if something had come up, she could have walked to the parking lot and explained what had delayed her. Maybe Roy was right; maybe something was really wrong.

"It's this one," Roy called, pointing to a neat white house on the corner of the block. He turned his bike into the drive and Nita followed.

"I will wait here while you go to the door?" Nita said, again making her statement sound like a question.

"No, you come with me. I've never met Sally's folks, and we might just as well meet them together."

"They do not go to church?" Nita asked.

"I've never seen them there," Roy replied. "Sally doesn't talk much about them either."

Roy rang the doorbell and stepped back to wait. The front door was open slightly, and he and Nita could hear talking going on inside.

"Well, why in the world aren't you out with that church bunch? You made a big enough scene about wanting to go." That was Sally's father, Roy was sure.

"Because I changed my mind," they heard Sally reply.

"Or maybe you mean your mother changed your mind."

"Would shomebody pleash get that doorbell."

"Oh, get it yourself, Barbara."

"Dad, can't you see? Mom's —" Sally's voice stopped abruptly.

"She's bombed. Sure I can see it. Is she ever any other way?"

Roy heard footsteps approaching, and soon a tall man opened the door.

"Yeah?" the man said.

For a minute Roy wasn't sure what he should say. He had been right—there was something very wrong at Sally's house.

"Is Sally here?" he asked softly. "My name's . . ."

"Sally," Mr. Benton turned and called loudly. "For you. Some kid and a girl."

Sally Benton shuddered as she spotted Roy and Nita standing in the doorway.

"What are you doing here?" she asked almost angrily.

"We were waiting for you at the church, Sally," Nita said kindly. "And when you did not show up, we decided to stop by and see if there was something wrong."

"Wrong? What could be wrong?" she snapped.

"Are these kids from the church?" Mr. Benton asked.

"Yes," Roy replied. "My name's Roy Sparton. We came to see if Sally was ready to go on the bike hike."

"I'm not going," Sally said briefly.

"You are going," her father snapped back.

"No, she's not," a slurred voice called from the other room. "I need Shally with me."

"You keep out of this, Barbara," Sally's father said, anger showing in his voice. "Now Sally, you get your things and get on your way."

"But Dad, can't you see? Mom needs me."

"Your mom doesn't need anything but her stupid bottle."

"Dad, please." Embarrassment showed in both her face and her voice.

Roy shifted from one foot to another.

"Oh, man, Sally, did we come at a bad time?" he asked sympathetically.

"Bad time?" Sally laughed strangely. "Frankly, it couldn't have been worse. Why didn't you just call?"

"We tried; I mean, we were going to, but the church was locked and we . . ."

"Oh, it wouldn't have made any difference. I guess you'd have to find out some time or other." Bitterness was evident in her voice.

"I am so sorry, Sally," Nita said with sincere concern.

"Shally, who are thesh people?" Mrs. Benton's voice sounded sleepy and almost incoherent.

"Just some kids from the church, Mom."

"Now, Sally," Mr. Benton injected. "You get your things like I said, and you go with these kids to that retreat or whatever it's called."

"No, Shally, pleash don't leave me alone."

11

"Don't pay any attention to your mother, Sally," Steve Benton spoke with deliberation. "I'll be here if she needs anything."

"Shure you'll be here—jush long enough for Shally to get away. And then you'll take off for the offish or shomeplace. And I'll be alone again."

"Maybe we should wait out in the yard by our bikes," Roy said, obviously embarrassed by the entire situation.

"No, just go on," Sally said loudly. "I'm not going."

"You are going," Steve Benton barked firmly. "I insist. Now get your gear, and get out of here."

Sally nodded to Roy and Nita that they should wait outside, and then she went to her room to get her things.

"Wow," Roy said, walking across the yard toward his bike. "I had no idea this was the kind of home Sally had."

Chapter 2

The Old Academy

Karen Tyler wasn't thinking about why Sally hadn't arrived at the church in time to leave with her group. All she was thinking about was the fact that Nita was in Roy's group. And she was stuck with a couple of strangers—kids she had never met before. Usually she liked meeting new people, but today it was different. It was bad enough that Roy seemed to like Sally Benton and that he didn't even realize that she, Karen Tyler, existed. But the fact that Nita was in his group was almost more than she could take.

Karen pumped along wearily, trying to carry on a conversation with the other two members of her team. But it just turned out to be a lot of empty words. When they arrived at the camp, she could team up with some of the kids she knew better. She hadn't seen some of them since last year's retreat, and she'd had only a few minutes to visit with them as they arrived at the church earlier.

*   *   *

Several miles back another threesome was just starting out.

"I hope I don't make us late," Sally said, knowing that if they were late it would be her fault—or her mother's.

13

"Naw, we've got lots of time," Roy answered confidently. "We set up the schedule so there'd be at least an hour before activities got under way."

"Oh, then we will have time to go and see that old castle you were telling me about?" Nita asked excitedly.

"Castle? Where is there a castle around here?" Sally asked in surprise.

"No, not a castle," Roy corrected. "An old academy."

"Oh, yes," Nita corrected herself. "That is what you said—an old academy. Can we go there?"

"What's so exciting about an old building?" Sally asked.

"I thought we might have our treasure hunt and singspiration there tonight," Roy said, turning to look at Sally as he talked. "But it's been such a long time since I was there, I thought I should go and check it out."

"So can we go there now?" Nita persisted.

"If Sally's game, I am," Roy answered, turning to see Sally's reaction.

"First I have to know what it's like," she said defensively.

"The academy? It's spooky and scary and deserted and—"

"And that's enough right there," Sally injected. "You just convinced me that I don't want to go, not alone."

"But you will not go alone," Nita explained quickly. "We will all three be together."

Sally frowned and turned to look at the German girl in dismay.

"You mean you like stuff like this?"

14

"Oh, yes," Nita replied. "It is interesting. Back in Germany there are many castles and buildings that are deserted. My friends and I used to explore them."

"See, Sally?" Roy laughed as he spoke. "Everybody likes things that are spooky."

"Not me!" Sally shuddered briefly. "I'm even afraid of a little old bug."

"Are there many bugs there?" Nita asked Roy.

"I s'pose," he replied. "This building hasn't been used for years, so I suppose there'd be some spiders and bugs and things."

"What do you mean by 'things'?" Sally asked quickly.

"Maybe snakes?" Nita made her statement sound like a question again.

"Snakes!" Sally screamed. "That does it. I'm not going."

Roy shook his head quickly. "No, I never saw any snakes out there."

"But you have not been there for a long time, no?" Nita persisted.

"That's right. But . . . well, I don't think there'd be snakes there." He was trying hard to convince Sally that she had nothing to worry about. But he knew the tall weeds and the old damp building were excellent places for just about anything—except people.

"How'd you ever find this place?" Sally asked, still not convinced that she should be following Roy to the deserted building.

Roy thought for a moment, recalling his childhood days when his father had been a pastor in the area.

"A bunch of us kids had a club. We'd go out

15

and explore things in every direction from town. But after we found the academy, we never went to any other place. We pretended it was our own secret hiding spot. Man, you wouldn't believe the stories we'd make up about it."

"Stories? What kind?" Sally persisted, hoping they would get her mind off the bugs and spiders that might confront her at the old building.

"Well, there are a bunch of huge rooms in this place. And we had heard how the guys went to school there and ate there and slept there and . . ." Roy paused, a smile playing on his lips.

"And what?"

"And if they didn't behave, they'd get thrown in the slammer down in the basement."

"Slammer. What is a slammer?" Nita asked seriously.

"It's like a prison or a jail," Roy replied.

"And this is where you want to take us?" Sally asked, a genuinely worried look on her face.

"Sure, are you game?"

"I am game," Nita answered immediately.

Roy turned to get Sally's reaction. "How about you, Sally?"

She hesitated for a brief moment. At least the excitement of the day was making her forget all the problems she had at home.

"Well, I guess," she managed. "At least if I see it now I won't be too shocked when we come back tonight."

"Good deal," Roy laughed. "You'll like it. I know you will."

"How far is it from camp?" Sally asked.

"Not far at all; just another direction." Roy

stopped his bike and looked at the tall weeds for a sign of a path.

"Man, these weeds have grown up. I don't think I'll ever find the real path, so let's just take off here."

"How will we know if we're in the right spot?" Sally asked, joking for the first time.

"I'm not sure," Roy answered. "But I can tell you this much—nobody's ever going to find this place unless someone is along who's been there before."

With that the three began riding their bikes into the tall weeded area. The girls followed Roy closely, hoping he knew where he was going.

"How much farther is it?" Nita asked. She wasn't used to riding a bike in high weeds.

"Not too much farther," Roy called back. "Should be seeing it soon."

"You mean you're still not sure where it is?" Sally questioned.

"Well, things have changed since I was here last." As he spoke he spotted the top of the old building. "Hey, there it is," he shouted. "See it?"

"Oh, yes," Nita called with excitement. "I see a chimney or something."

"That's it," Roy said. "Come on, follow me."

Reluctantly, Sally followed Nita and Roy as they dodged the tall weeds and broken tree branches in the overgrown path.

"There!" Roy said jubilantly. "There she is. Now isn't that something?"

"Something I'm still not sure I want to explore," Sally insisted.

"Sally, you will like it once you forget about all the spiders and bugs and things."

17

"Nita! I *had* forgotten until you reminded me just now."

"Let's put our bikes down here." Roy pointed to a spot near the old building. "And you can leave your packs and stuff here too."

"But won't someone come and steal them?" Nita asked seriously.

"Nobody will ever be able to find them, let alone steal them," Sally said in mock disgust.

Roy agreed. "You're right, Sally. No danger of anything being stolen. Not even a chance anybody will find this hideout."

"Oh, Roy, that's twice you've said that. That makes me feel uneasy," Sally managed.

"You are afraid, Sally?" the German girl asked.

"Well, no, not exactly afraid, just...just..."

"Just scared to death, huh, Sally?" Roy teased.

"Oh, Roy, you're sure no help."

"Here; right up here," Roy said, leading his two companions up the cracked cement steps and through a large entrance. Then cupping his hands to his mouth, he shouted loudly, "Hello." His voice reverberated through the empty building. "Man, isn't that echo neat?"

"Oh, yes, it almost makes me lonesome for Germany," Nita said. "We have many large empty buildings standing since the war. My father used to take me to see them when I was young."

"Well, this place is sure deserted," Roy agreed. "I figured we could have our treasure hunt around here." Then pointing to various sections of the large room, he said, "This is a great place for our singspiration and refreshments. Neat, huh?"

"Yeah, neat, Roy," Sally said, wrinkling up

18

her nose and looking at all the dust and spider webs. "Real neat. Now, let's get out of here."

"Not yet, Sally," Roy spoke with firmness. "There are still a bunch of rooms and things I want to show you."

"Oh, yes," Nita added. "You haven't taken us to the spooky places yet."

Roy clicked his heels and turned.

"Just follow me, ladies. You haven't seen anything yet."

Sally shuddered. But there was one thing for sure: She wasn't going to stay in this room alone. She followed her friends.

Chapter 3

Pastor Don Calls

Pastor Don finished unloading the last of the boxes of food and equipment from the church van. He paused to look at his watch for the third time. Roy should have been there long ago. He was supposed to get the activities started. But instead, he was probably waiting at the church for Sally Benton. It was obvious to almost everyone around that the young pastor was disgusted.

Karen Tyler was trying to concentrate on a Ping Pong game with some of her friends. But watching Pastor Don and wondering when Nita would come bouncing in with Roy and Sally took most of her attention.

"Come on, Karen," one of the fellows said. "Get with it."

Before she could answer, Pastor Don came into the rec room. "Anyone have any idea where Roy Sparton is?"

Nobody answered audibly, but several shrugged their shoulders or shook their heads.

Karen had wondered too. It wasn't like Roy to be late for anything, and if he was in charge, you could sure count on him to take his responsibility seriously. Even when other kids neglected their jobs, Roy would take over so that things would get done on time.

"Where's his sister?" the pastor asked, looking straight at Karen.

21

"She's decorating the dining room," Karen answered lamely. She wasn't sure what Joy would have to do with Roy's not showing up, but she didn't think she should ask.

"Dash down there and ask her if she knows what happened to that twin brother of hers," the youth pastor ordered.

"Pastor Don," Karen said, putting down her Ping Pong paddle. "Joy wouldn't know anything about him. She was in the first group to leave, remember?"

Pastor Don nodded, disgust still showing on his face. "Well, who would know?"

Karen thought for a minute. "Maybe you should call the church and see if Roy's still there."

"Still there? He wouldn't stick around and wait for Sally for an hour." He paused significantly and then asked, "Would he?"

"I don't know," Karen said loud enough for everyone to hear. "He's really got a thing for Sally Benton. And he'd probably do 'most anything where she was involved."

The others laughed, but Pastor Don was not amused. "You've got to be kidding! An hour?" With that, he turned and started for the pay telephone booth.

He took several steps before returning. "I just remembered; there's no one at the church. It's locked up. Roy couldn't get to that phone, even if he heard it ringing."

Karen shrugged her shoulders. "Was he still there when you left?"

The youth pastor nodded. "Yeah, but I told him not to stick around too long."

Karen waited almost a minute before offering another suggestion. "Maybe you should call Sally's house and find out what time she left. That might give you some clues."

"Sounds like a good idea," the pastor agreed. "Do you have her phone number?"

Without a moment's hesitation, Karen rattled off the number.

For the first time in several minutes the youth pastor smiled. He pulled a pen and a piece of paper from his pocket and wrote down the number. "You gals have it all over us when it comes to telephone numbers. I should have known you would have it memorized." With that he strode toward the phone booth. Suddenly he stopped again and turned to face Karen.

"Thanks, Karen. And forgive me for jumping down your throat. It isn't your fault. I'm sorry."

"That's OK, Pastor Don. I'm a little disgusted with those three myself."

"Who else was in that group?" the pastor asked, trying to remember who had been at the church when he left.

"Nita."

"Nita? The German girl who lives at your place?"

"Right," Karen said simply.

Pastor Don wiped the perspiration from his forehead. "Boy, I hope they haven't run into any problems."

Karen replied, "I doubt that they have. I think Roy just decided he'd wait for Sally, that's all."

The pastor shook his head, but he said

23

nothing. Instead, he dialed the number Karen had given him and waited for the phone to ring.

*   *   *

At the Benton house, Steve and Barbara were still barking out harsh words to each other. It had been that way most of the morning. In fact, it had been that way most of the time ever since the family had found out about Mrs. Benton's drinking problem. Only the shrill sound of the telephone stopped the unkind words from flying about the room.

"Get that phone," Barbara screamed from her favorite chair in the den. "I'sh driving me nutsh."

Steve stared bitterly at his wife and walked silently to the kitchen to pick up the phone.

"Hello," he snapped as though the caller was to blame for the situation in his home.

"Mr. Benton?"

"Speaking."

"Mr. Benton, this is Pastor Don. Is Sally there?"

"No, she's at some church thing this weekend and won't be home until Sunday night."

"Well, could you tell me what time she left?"

"Oh, it must have been about—Who'd you say this was?"

"Pastor Don—from the camp."

Steve's face suddenly turned pale, and his voice rose sharply. "Well, isn't Sally there?"

"No, her group hasn't arrived yet. I knew they got a little late start, so I thought I'd call and . . ."

Steve broke in deliberately. "They left more than an hour ago."

"Well, that's what I wanted to find out. Roy Sparton was supposed to get things set up, and he hasn't shown up, so . . ."

"Hang Roy Sparton. What's happened to my daughter?"

With that Barbara Benton straightened in her chair. Even in her drunken condition she understood that something was very wrong. She could tell by her husband's words and by the tone of his voice.

"Whash happen to Shally?" she called from the den.

"Oh, you keep out of this, will you?" Steve barked back.

"Beg your pardon?" replied Pastor Don.

"Not you, my wife."

"Oh," was all the young pastor said.

Steve knew that the conversation was confusing to the caller, but he did nothing to clear it up.

"I wanna know whash happen to my Shally," Barbara Benton persisted.

"Barbara, knock it off, will ya? I'm trying to talk to this jerk from the camp." Then he realized what he had called the young minister. "Sorry, nothing personal," he mumbled.

"That's OK. I'm sorry, too, Mr. Benton. I probably shouldn't have called and upset everyone there. They'll no doubt be here in a few minutes."

"Well, they'd better be. And if they don't show up in about ten minutes, you call me back. Understand?"

"Yes, sir. I'll do that."

"In fact, if they're not there in five minutes, you let me know. I'll call the police."

25

"Oh, I'm sure it's nothing serious, sir."

"Don't you tell me if it's serious or not. This is *my* daughter we're talking about. And if something has happened to her, I'll hold you responsible. Get that?"

By this time Barbara Benton had found her way into the kitchen and was hanging on to her husband's arm. "Whasha matter with Shally," she said again and again.

"Nothing. Just keep out of this." With that Steve slammed down the receiver and turned to leave the room.

"Oh, no you don't Shteve Benton," she said, trying to keep him from leaving. "You jush tell me what the man shaid about Shally."

"Nothing," Steve snapped loudly. "He's just excited over nothing. Stupid church people anyway."

"Nothing?" Barbara belched.

Steve jerked away from his wife angrily. "I said nothing. Now go on back to your bottle; that's all you need anyway."

"You made Shally go on that thing, Shteve. You forched her to go, even when I shaid she should shtay here. Remember?"

"Barbara. You button your lip before I do it for you. I've had about all the nonsense I'm going to take from you today." He tried to get through the doorway, but his wife put her arms across the opening.

"But you made her go, Shteve. You did it."

Steve Benton's patience came to an end, and he swore angrily at his wife.

"I told you, I've had all I can take from you today. There's probably nothing wrong with Sally.

26

They must just have had some bike trouble—a flat tire or something. That's all."

The lame excuse offered by Steve Benton was no comfort to Sally's mother.

"You don't believe that for one minute, Shteve." The words still slurred recklessly from her mouth. "If you did, you wouden wanna call the policesh."

"I just said that to give that stupid preacher a scare, that's all."

Barbara Benton grabbed her husband's arm again and anger flashed in her eyes. The speech that had been so slurred only seconds before suddenly seemed to clear considerably. Her voice rose in fear and anger.

"You, Steve Benton, are to blame for all this. If something has happened to my Sally, I'll never forgive you. Never, never, never. Do you hear?" With that, she burst into uncontrollable sobbing.

Chapter 4

Trapped!

Sally Benton managed to duck and miss most of the spider webs in the old academy building, but she was still not convinced that it would be a good place for the retreat group to have a party.

"That's because you haven't seen the best part of the building," Roy chided. "Just wait until I take you down to the old prison. Now that's really something to see."

"What is down there?" Nita asked.

"Nothing, really; just some dark, cold rooms. I was just kidding."

"But I would like to see them, wouldn't you, Sally?" Nita said with real enthusiasm.

Sally wasn't sure she wanted to stick around the dirty old building much longer, but her attitude changed noticeably when Roy began to tell about his childhood ambition to chin himself on the old prison gate.

"All the kids in the club had done it," he said.

"And did you do it too?" Nita asked.

"Nope. I was always too short. Couldn't reach it."

"And they let you be a member of the club anyway?" Sally asked.

"They had to; I was the one who found this building."

"But you never accomplished that great feat!"

29

Sally said, joking for the first time since coming into the old building.

"Nope; never could reach the dumb thing."

Their laughter filled the old Army academy and echoed through the halls and rooms.

"Well, you're not too short now," Sally challenged.

"You mean you want me to go down there and chin myself?"

"I'll even go down and cheer for you."

"Hey, that's a deal! OK with you, Nita?"

"Oh, yes, of course. I wanted to see the prison but did not think Sally would want to go down there."

"Only if Roy chins himself," Sally affirmed.

"I said it's a deal. But watch your step. The floor down there is pretty beat up."

"Did someone beat up the floor?" Nita asked seriously.

At that Sally laughed heartily, forgetting for a moment her fears about the bugs and spiders.

"Oh, Nita, I guess we say a lot of funny things," Sally said. "But just stick around with us, and you'll soon understand what we're talking about."

"Yeah," Roy said, still laughing. "What I meant was that the building is in pretty bad condition."

"Why did you not say that? Then I would have understood you," Nita defended herself.

"You're right," Roy said, nodding slowly. "We've talked this way so long, we just think everyone knows what we mean."

"Well, I do now. The building is beat up in bad shape. Right?"

"Right," Roy and Sally answered together, still laughing at their friend.

For the first time since Sally had entered the old Army academy, she seemed to be enjoying herself. She had not only forgotten her unhappy family situation, but she had also forgotten about the bugs and spiders. She teased Roy unmercifully about being too heavy now rather than too short to chin himself. The old gate probably would not hold him.

"Too heavy?" Roy said defensively. "The coach tells me I've got to put on a few pounds if I expect to make the team next year."

Roy continued to lead the way down the darkened hallway. Suddenly, Sally let out a scream.

"What happened?" Roy asked, shock in his voice. "You trip?"

"No, something went crawling by my foot—like a rat or mouse or something."

"Oh, man, Sally. I guess there would be mice and rats in an old building like this."

"Well, I can tell you this," Sally said pointedly. "If a rat comes anywhere near me, I'll faint dead away. I'm scared to death of those things."

"Do they attack people?" Nita wanted to know.

"I've read that they sometimes bite, but we'll just watch for them and get out of here if we see any."

"Well, I think I've already seen one," Sally retorted.

Roy turned to face her.

"So do you want to leave, or do you want to see Roy Sparton chin himself?"

31

Sally relaxed a little and agreed to stay for the exhibition.

"Well, here are the old cell blocks," Roy said, taking the girls into the prison area.

"This is where they put the naughty men?" Nita asked.

"That's it," Roy said, enjoying Nita's choice of words. "This is where they put the naughty men, all right."

"And this is the old gate you couldn't reach?" Sally asked, pointing to one of the prison gates that stood open.

"This is the one," he confessed. Raising his arms, he touched the top of the door. "Man, I can practically reach it without jumping now."

There was a twinkle in Sally's eyes, but Roy could not see it because of the semidarkness in the room.

"Just think," Sally joked. "When the *Daily News* hears about this, they'll want to come down and take pictures and print it in the morning edition. 'Roy Sparton Finally Chins Himself on Prison Gate.'"

"Well, they should," Roy boasted. "It's been a lifetime ambition that has never been fulfilled—until now."

"You haven't done it yet," Sally reminded him.

"OK, girls, step aside; here goes." Roy flexed his muscles in preparation for the task.

"I wish I'd brought my camera," Sally teased.

"I have mine out with my bike," Nita added. "But I did not take it with me because I did not know there was going to be such an important event take place."

Roy jumped up, grabbed the top of the prison gate and slowly chinned himself.

"How's that?" he asked, lowering himself again.

"That was wonderful, Roy. I'll never regret coming down here to witness this great event," Sally said as seriously as she could.

"Anyone else want to try?" Roy asked in mock seriousness.

"Not me," Sally said with determination. "I'm still watching for rats."

"Maybe they have gone away by now," Nita said. But even as she spoke, she glanced from one side of the cell to the other, silently admitting to Sally that she was not as brave as she had pretended to be.

"Well, now that we've taken care of all the important things," Roy said, "maybe we'd better head for camp."

"Well, at least we can tell the others what an exciting place this is for the party," Nita said jubilantly.

"You can tell them that, but I'm not sure I will," confessed Sally.

"Really? Didn't you like it?" Roy had hoped that Sally would have changed her mind by now.

"Not really. Too many scary things."

"Like rats and dark hallways and stuff?"

"Yeah."

"But that is what makes a place spooky," Nita added. "It will be a good place for the treasure hunt, I think."

As she spoke, all three suddenly heard a soft scurrying sound.

33

"That rat's around here again; I'm getting out of here," Sally screamed.

With that she turned quickly. As she did, she hit the large handle of the gate with her arm and the sound of clanking metal echoed throughout the building.

"What happened?" Sally asked, still somewhat in shock.

"I don't know. I heard something fall." Roy walked over to the big gate to look around.

"I thought I heard something else fall before," Nita said. "When you jumped up on the gate to chin yourself."

"You did?" Roy was surprised. He had been so intent on showing off for the girls that he had heard nothing.

"This piece." Nita stooped to pick up a small piece of metal from the floor. Roy took the piece in his fingers and then turned to give the gate a push. It wouldn't budge. He stood there stunned.

"Come on, Roy, let's get out of here," Sally insisted.

"I think we're trapped," he said softly.

"Trapped? What do you mean?"

Roy gave the gate another push. "I can't get the gate open."

"You're kidding, I hope," Sally said loudly.

"I wish I was." The crack in his voice told Sally and Nita that he was serious—very serious.

"You mean we are stuck in the slammer?" Nita said, trying to remember the words Roy had used.

"I think so," Roy admitted, laughing briefly at Nita's description.

"Roy, this is no time for joking," Sally scolded. "Are we really trapped here with all these spiders and rats and things?"

"I wish I was kidding," Roy said soberly. "But honest, Sally, we're trapped in this building. Look." With that he gave the gate another firm jerk, but it would not budge.

"What happened to it?" Nita wanted to know, not fully convinced that they had become prisoners in the old deserted Army building.

Roy took the small metal piece and showed the girls where it had fit into the lock. "It looks like this thing rusted out, and the little lever that's suppose to hold it must have broken."

"When I fell on it?" Sally asked.

"Either then or when I chinned myself on it." He laughed momentarily. "Maybe you were right, Sally, about my being too heavy now."

"Roy, please do not tease us," Nita said. "Are you serious?"

"I'm as serious as I've ever been, Nita. We're trapped." He paused and turned the small piece of metal in his hand again and again. "Boy, do I ever wish I was teasing."

"Can we not call for help?" Nita asked.

"I don't think anybody will hear us. Don't you remember how far we came from the road?" Roy asked numbly.

"But our bikes are out there. Someone will see them and send help, will they not?" Nita continued, searching desperately for some way out.

"Nobody comes out here, Nita," Roy repeated.

"Nobody even knows this dumb place exists," Sally grumbled.

"I'm sorry, Sally. I really didn't mean to do this to you."

"But it is not your fault, Roy," Nita said, trying to defend him. "We all wanted to come."

"Sally didn't. I talked her into it."

"No, you didn't," Sally said. "I was the one who challenged you to come down here and chin yourself, remember?"

The German girl turned to face her friend. "Maybe I was the one who influenced you, Sally. I wanted so very much to see the prison Roy had talked about. I am sorry."

Roy Sparton dropped the rusty piece of metal to the floor. "Look, we can't each take the blame this way," Roy said, trying to cheer his companions. "Let me try this thing again. Maybe I just did it wrong." But the gate failed to move. They really were trapped in the old Army academy prison.

"But someone will find us, maybe?" Nita asked, searching for some kind of encouragement.

"I sure hope so," Sally managed. "We'll just have to pray that they will."

"Maybe someone will come to this building to check it or something," Nita suggested.

"No chance," Roy said, discouragement showing in his voice.

"Do they not come and cut the weeds—or something?" Nita's voice faded to a whisper.

"Sure doesn't look like they've done too great a job on that up to now," Sally replied with disgust.

"That's for sure," Roy commented.

"I think I am beginning to be afraid," Nita said softly.

"Oh, man, Nita, I really am sorry—and Sally." Roy's voice was very unsteady. "I shouldn't have taken you here in the first place. I should have

36

taken you right to the camp and come back by myself later."

As he spoke, Sally Benton slumped ungracefully to the floor. "Sally," Roy and Nita cried together. "Sally, what happened?" But the girl lay speechless on the hard concrete cell floor.

Chapter 5

Search Parties

Karen Tyler lined up with the other campers, waiting for instructions from Pastor Don. They had decided to form a search party, and all those who lived within ten miles of the area were to look for the missing campers. The others were encouraged to stay on the campground and pray for God's guidance in the search.

The group sang a prayer chorus and then went their separate ways. Karen joined Joy and one of the boys from the church.

"Roy used to go to some old building out this way when he was a kid," Joy said as the three left the area. "I have no idea where it is, but I know he used to go out there a lot."

"But why in the world would he want to go to an old building now?" Karen asked. "He was supposed to be at camp."

"Maybe he planned to take the kids out there later or something," Joy suggested. "He's always looking for surprises to spring on people."

"Well," said the boy who accompanied them, "we'd better not waste our time looking for a building; let's just look for the kids."

With that they separated, walking some 50

feet apart, carefully searching the weeded area within walking distance of the campground.

* * *

Steve Benton paced nervously from the living room to the kitchen, waiting for the telephone to ring. His wife had managed to get to the kitchen, and Steve had fixed her some coffee to help her sober up more quickly.

"That guy should be calling by now," he stormed loudly, even though only the two of them were in the room. "His five minutes is up. What's the matter with him?"

Barbara stared at her husband hatefully, but said nothing. Sally would be home right now if Steve hadn't insisted that she go on that retreat. He had practically pushed her out of the house. And look what had happened. Her Sally was missing or lost or maybe even—. She couldn't make herself think the word. The shrill ring of the telephone brought her back to reality. Steve grabbed the receiver and, without saying hello, blurted out his concern.

"Have you found her yet?" he asked forcefully.

"No, Mr. Benton," said Pastor Don. "But we've formed search parties and . . ."

"Search parties!" Steve yelled in anger. "What do a bunch of church kids know about searching?"

"These are kids who live in the area," the pastor explained. "And the rest of the campers are staying here to pray—"

Steve did not let him finish.

"Pray!" he shouted. "Well, you get off this line right now so I can call the police. Pray," he repeated distastefully. With that he slammed the receiver down, picked up the telephone book and began to leaf through the pages. He turned to the back section of the book.

"Tyler. That's who I'll call. Tyler."

"Who's Tyler?" Barbara asked.

"Sally's friend, Karen. You know her. Well, her father . . ." Steve looked at his wife to see if she was getting what he was saying. She seemed sober enough, but he couldn't be sure. "Bob Tyler tried to convert me once, but . . ."

"Too bad he didn't succeed," Barbara interrupted. "Maybe we'd have a good home now."

"Look who's talking." Steve's voice filled with hatred and anger again. Deep down in his heart he blamed himself for Sally's disappearance. His wife was right. He had insisted that Sally go on the retreat, but he had done it to get her away from her mother and this terrible situation. Or had he? If he would face up to the truth, he'd probably admit that he sent her away just to show his wife who was boss. He dialed the Tyler number and then waited impatiently for someone to answer.

"Tyler? Steve Benton here. I need you to help me find Sally."

The voice on the other end expressed surprise. "You need what?"

"Sally. She's missing, and I want you to go with me to look for her."

"Well, sure, Steve. What happened?" Concern showed in his question.

"Let's not take time for that now; just meet me here at my house." He rattled off the address, put the receiver back on the phone and resumed his pacing. Strange that he should have thought about Bob Tyler right now. But Tyler had told him

41

to call if he ever needed him, and boy, did he need his help now.

"And where do you think you and this Tyler are going to find Sally?" Barbara said, spitting out the words angrily.

Steve spoke just as harshly. "I don't know, but we'll follow the road they took and—"

Barbara broke in with more fury: "Sally wouldn't be lost now if you hadn't forced her to leave. You know that."

"I know, I know," Steve snapped. "You've told me a thousand times. Now get off my back, will you?"

But Sally's mother ignored his remarks. "She didn't want to go. You know that, too, don't you, Steve? She didn't want to go."

"She *did* want to go," he screamed. "You just made her feel guilty about leaving you."

"I didn't make her feel guilty, she —" Barbara stopped suddenly when she saw the Tyler car pull up to the curb.

Without a word to his wife Steve left the house quickly, slamming the door behind him.

"Jump in," Bob Tyler said.

"No, you park your car in our drive," Steve called back. "I'll drive. I've lived around here all my life; I know the area better than you do."

Tyler followed Steve's orders, and in almost no time at all the Benton car pulled away from the curb.

"Sure took you long enough to get here," Steve snapped at his companion.

"Sorry about that. I got caught in traffic. When did Sally disappear? I thought maybe she'd

42

be going to the retreat with the other kids from church."

Steve explained that Sally had left for camp. "But some guy—Pastor Don, I think it was—called and said she and a couple of other kids had never arrived. Nobody knows where Sally might be."

"Well, they surely are between here and the camp somewhere. Didn't your wife want to go along with us?" Bob Tyler asked.

Steve laughed sarcastically. "My wife?" he said bitterly. "She'd only be in the way."

"But I'll bet she's as worried as you are, Steve."

"Worried? She's got her booze to keep her steady."

Bob Tyler did not comment on that. "I wonder if we should pull over and have prayer before we get too far?"

"Prayer?" Steve spit out the word with disdain. "I'm not stopping for that. If you want to pray, just go ahead."

"OK, I think I will. You know, God hears us wherever we are."

"Well, we wouldn't have to be praying if that church bunch had handled things the way they should have."

"Oh? How's that?"

"Well, anybody knows kids need supervision."

"They did have supervision, Steve. Pastor Don went along."

"Then how'd those kids get lost?"

"I don't have the answer to that. But God does."

"All you ever do is talk religion, Tyler. Now if you're going to pray, then pray."

"All right."

As Bob Tyler bowed his head, Steve watched him from the corner of his eye. He didn't have too much use for religion, but he sure hoped God would come to their assistance this time.

"Dear Lord," Bob Tyler started softly, "I come to you today on behalf of these young people who are missing. I know that You know where they are, and I pray that You will keep your hand of protection on them. Thank you that they are Your children and that we can commit them to You. We trust You now for guidance. In Jesus name, amen."

Steve Benton cleared his throat nervously.

"And that's going to do the trick?" he asked with suspicion.

"What trick, Steve?"

"Finding Sally." As he spoke his voice cracked slightly.

"Well, I don't know about tricking God into anything, but I'm certainly glad that I can tell Him how I feel during a time like this."

"I guess I didn't exactly mean 'trick,'" Steve responded more quietly. "I meant, well, you seem to count so much on praying."

"Oh, I do," Bob Tyler said confidently. "But not especially on the praying, but on the Lord who answers prayer."

Steve drove on quietly for some time. Religion wasn't exactly his thing, but it sure seemed to be Bob Tyler's thing, and Sally's too. Maybe a little of it wouldn't hurt the family. Maybe if they'd had it, Barbara wouldn't be an alcoholic now. Well, if God would answer Bob Tyler's prayer, maybe even he, Steve Benton, would start going to church. That's it; he'd make a deal with God. If God would help

44

them find Sally, he'd start going to church. He shared his thoughts with Bob Tyler as they rode on.

"That's no good," Bob replied.

"What do you mean 'no good.' I told you I'd start going to church."

"But God doesn't make deals, Steve."

"Well, that's the way I do business. If God shows us where Sally is and if she's OK, then you'll see me in church next Sunday."

"You're giving God orders, Steve? You're telling the Creator and Saviour of the world to fall in line with your plans?"

"Oh, come on, Bob. You know that's not what I said."

"It sounded that way to me, Steve."

Before they could finish their conversation Steve called out, "Hey, there's someone."

"That's Karen," Bob Tyler said. "My daughter."

"What's she doing out here?"

"I don't know; let's stop and find out."

Steve Benton pulled the car over to the side of the road. "Make it short, Tyler. Remember, we're still looking for *my* daughter, not yours."

Bob Tyler rolled down the car window. "Karen," he called. "Karen."

"Dad!" Karen showed her surprise in meeting her father. "What are you doing out—oh, Mr. Benton, hi. We're looking for Roy and Sally and Nita," she explained before they could ask.

"You think she's out this way?" Steve said, ignoring the fact that Karen had mentioned all three of the missing young people.

"We don't know," she said a little breathless.

45

"But Roy's sister said he used to come out this way when he was a kid. I think there was some kind of deserted building or something that he went to, and she thought we should try to find it and —"

"The Army academy?" Steve asked. "Is that where they are?"

"I don't know, but —"

Steve did not let her finish. "Come on, Tyler. I know where that is. My dad used to take me there when I was a kid."

"Karen, you and your friends keep looking," Bob Tyler said as the car began to pull away. "We'll keep in touch."

Steve Benton sped away and turned the wheel as he approached a sharp curve.

"Is there a road to this place?" Bob questioned.

"Not on this side, but there is on the other."

"How far is that?" Bob asked, concerned about the way Steve was driving.

"Less than ten miles."

For the next several minutes the car sped along the gravel road. Steve drove much faster than Bob Tyler would have if he had been driving.

"Better slow down a bit, Steve," he warned, "or we may not be around to find Sally and the others."

"I know this road like a book," he boasted. "The road to the academy is just on the other side of this curve. See, there it is."

Bob Tyler looked the direction Steve was pointing. There was a road all right, but there was also a sign in front of it: ROAD CLOSED. BRIDGE WASHED OUT.

Chapter 6

"My Baby'sh Mishing"

Back in her little white house in Trendale, Barbara Benton paced nervously from the kitchen to the front entrance. After all the coffee Steve had forced her to drink, she walked more steadily than she had earlier. The effect of the liquor she had consumed was wearing off. But she was worried, really worried, and she was sure that only another drink could make her feel better.

Something had happened to Sally. If only Steve had told her what that telephone conversation had been all about, she might not be so concerned. But she knew almost nothing except that Sally had never arrived at the camp. She shook her head. Steve knew what had happened, and he was worried. That had been obvious from the time the first call had come from the camp director.

Maybe Sally had been hit by a car. Barbara stopped walking. No, it couldn't be that or the camp people would have told Steve and he would have been on his way to the hospital. It was something else. Maybe she had been kidnapped. Oh, why hadn't Steve given her the details?

She knew why. It was because she was drunk, and he knew she wouldn't have got the story straight even if he had told her.

Barbara turned suddenly and headed for the kitchen. She could call the camp director and find out for herself. But even as she reached for the

47

phone, she knew that idea would never work. She not only didn't know the number of the camp, she didn't even know the name of it. It had something to do with the church, she knew, but what? Why hadn't she shown more interest and asked Sally about the retreat?

The more Barbara Benton thought about the entire situation, the more angry she became at her husband. She could still remember the shouting and name-calling that had gone on a few hours before. No wonder Sally had decided to go to the retreat. She wanted to get out of this awful house.

No, that wasn't it, Barbara told herself. Sally was afraid of her father—that's why she had left.

The more Barbara tried to reason out the facts, the more depressed and confused she became. Suddenly she began to weep, shaking uncontrollably. Walking again to the front entrance, she cried aloud, "Oh, Sally, my baby. Where are you, honey?"

Staring out the glass in the door, she saw a patrol car cruise by the house. The police—that was it! She had distinctly heard Steve tell the camp director that he was going to call the police. Maybe she could find out from them what had happened. They would tell her, especially when they found out she was Sally's mother.

Quickly she returned to the kitchen. As she passed the refrigerator, she thought of the tall brown liquor bottle inside. She knew it was right there in the front section where she could get it anytime she had the urge for a drink—day or night. She looked up at the clock. It had been hours since she'd had a drink, or at least it seemed that way. And as upset and nervous as she was right

48

now, a drink was the only thing that could help her, she was sure of that.

"Just one drink," she told herself. "Just one small drink."

She took the bottle from the refrigerator and sat down on a kitchen chair to pour herself a drink. As she did, she reasoned that nobody would really blame her for what she was doing. After all, her Sally was lost. She poured another drink and then another. How many more she drank she didn't really know—or care. She just wanted to get even with Steve.

"Shteve knows whash's wrong," she said aloud, "but he won't tell me."

Cradling the bottle in her hands, she bumped the glass with her elbow. It rolled off the table and crashed to the floor. The sound of the breaking glass seemed to bring clearer thoughts to her mind.

"The policsh," she said, finally remembering why she had come back to the kitchen. "I'm gonna call the policsh. They'll tell me where my Shally ish."

Barbara picked up the telephone book and began carelessly leafing through the pages. Every now and then she would stop to glance at a page and run her finger down the columns of names and numbers. But it was no use; she couldn't discern one number from another.

Taking the telephone in her hands, she dialed the operator. A friendly voice came through clearly.

"May I help you, please?"

The sound of the crisp voice startled Barbara momentarily.

49

"I need the policsh," she said. "Can you get me the policsh?"

"Is this an emergency?" the operator questioned.

"Emergency? Yesh!" cried Barbara. "My baby'sh mishing."

"One moment, please."

Barbara waited for what seemed many moments, but soon a voice broke into her troubled thoughts.

"Officer Ryan here. May I help you?"

"No," Barbara shouted. "I want the policsh."

"Madam," said the officer calmly, "this is the police."

Barbara was still disturbed by the officer's easy-going attitude and wondered if the operator had really connected her with the police department. But right now there was no way she could find another number, so this man would have to do, she told herself.

"May I help you?" the officer repeated.

"Yesh," Barbara cried. "My baby'sh mishing. Shomething happen to my Shally."

"Your baby?" the officer asked. "Your baby's missing?"

"Shally's losht," Mrs. Benton repeated, not realizing that her thick-sounding speech made it difficult for the officer to understand her. He continued to ask more questions.

"Madam," he said evenly. "I think you've been drinking. And —"

"You think I'm jusht a drunk?" Barbara asked, hardly able to say the words clearly enough to be understood. "I'm not; I'm jusht worried about my Shally."

50

"Could I have your name and address?" he asked. "I'll send an officer to your home to get all the needed information."

"You don't need any more information," Barbara cried, tears coursing down her cheeks. "I've told you—my Shally is losht, and I want you to find her."

"Yes, Ma'am," the officer said.

"And her father'sh losht too," she added.

"The father is missing as well as the baby?" the officer questioned.

"What baby?" asked Barbara, stunned by the officer's inquiry. "I don't know anything about a mishing baby. I jusht know that Shally's losht, and her father won't tell me what'sh going on."

"Her father is there?" the officer asked, still confused.

Barbara mumbled her reply. "No, Shteve'sh not here. He went to look for Shally. And now they're both gone."

Then she heard the officer call to another member of the force: "Finely, did you get a trace on this call yet?"

"Got it, Sarge."

"Tell you what, Madam," said the officer. "You stay right there, and we'll send someone to your home to give you a little help. All right?"

"I don't need no help. I jusht want my Shally," Barbara continued.

"Well, we'll see what we can do," the officer replied and hung up.

Barbara held the receiver in her hands a long time after the police officer had hung up. What had that man been talking about—a missing baby? Maybe some other mother had called too.

"Poor thing," Barbara said aloud. "She losht her baby too."

With that she stood cautiously and walked slowly into the den and sat down in her favorite chair, staring hard at the floor. Suddenly she began to cry, softly at first, tears trickling down her swollen cheeks. Soon she was sobbing uncontrollably.

Sally was lost; Sally—the only reason she even wanted to live. Her little girl was lost. Maybe she would never be found.

"O God," Barbara cried, not realizing that she was actually praying. "O God, don't let anything happen to my Shally."

She buried her head in her hands and continued to sob out her distress.

Chapter 7

Nita Believes

"Sally, what's the matter?" Roy asked, bending over her and trying to rouse her.

"I think she has fainted," said Nita, bending down with him.

"What would make her do a thing like that?" Roy's voice rose until it almost squeaked.

"I do not know, unless. . ." Nita's shaky voice proved that she was frightened.

"Boy, I've never been with anyone who's fainted," Roy said. "What should we do?"

Nita looked around as though she was searching for something.

"I think most of the time people use smelling salts."

"Smelling salts? But we don't have any."

"Sometimes they splash water in the face," she continued.

"And that's another thing we don't have."

As he spoke, Sally began to stir.

"Hey, she's coming to—I think."

"Wow," Sally said, trying to sit up. "What happened?"

"I guess you fainted or something," Roy said lamely, helping her up.

"Oh, now I remember. The rat."

"A rat?" Roy could hardly believe what he was hearing.

"Yes, he looked like he was coming straight for

53

me. I got scared and tried to jump out of the way. And that's all I remember."

"Well, are you OK now?" Roy asked, wondering if there was something he should be doing for her. "I mean, do you feel all right?"

"Yeah, I think so. What happened to the rat?"

"I don't know; I didn't even see it," Roy said.

"Well, you can take my word for it," Sally assured him. "It was here."

"Maybe he has gone already," Nita said, trying to offer a word of comfort.

"Lucky for him," Roy mumbled. "Wish it was that easy for us to get out."

"Boy, something must have happened to my arm," Sally said, rubbing it gingerly. "I guess I hit it on the gate handle."

"Here, let me see."

Even in the semidarkness of the prison Roy could tell that Sally's arm was red and swollen.

"I wish I had a first aid kit here. Then we could clean off that scratch and bandage it up," he offered.

"I'm sort of glad you don't," Sally said. "I'm such a chicken about things like that, I'd probably faint again."

"I hope you will be feeling all right, Sally," Nita said with deep concern.

"I'll feel great just as soon as we get out of here."

Roy cringed at her statement. "Sally, that gate is locked, remember? Really locked."

"Then we'll just have to pray and ask the Lord to help us get out some other way."

This statement surprised Nita. "You mean God will open the door if we pray?"

"Well, maybe not exactly open it automatically," she admitted. "But we can count on God to help us, I know that." Sally rubbed her arm as she spoke.

"Hey, you remember our Sunday school lesson last week?" Roy brightened as he spoke.

"Yeah, it was about Paul and Silas," Sally said. "And they were in prison."

"Like we are?" Nita offered.

"And the gate was locked too," Roy said, pointing to the big gate that had made them unwilling prisoners in the academy.

"But they sang and praised the Lord," Sally added.

"How could they do that?" Nita wanted to know.

"Because they knew God was with them," Roy assured her.

"And God is with us too," Sally said confidently. "So why don't we praise the Lord like they did?"

"You mean sing?" Nita could hardly believe what she was hearing.

"Sure. And we can say some Bible verses too," Sally suggested.

"Bible verses?" Nita was really confused.

"Yeah, let's take turns saying verses that mean something special to us; that is, if you feel up to it, Sally." Roy's concern for his friend was obvious.

"Oh, sure, I'm OK—except for my arm."

"I do not really know very many Bible verses," Nita confessed.

"Well, just think about the ones you memorized when you were in church. You can say them in

German if you want. God understands all languages," Roy suggested.

"But I did not memorize Bible verses in my church."

"You didn't?"

"Not that I remember, except in my catechism class."

"Well, say those."

"I do not remember any of those either."

"But what about those you learned when you accepted the Lord?" Sally asked.

"Accepted the Lord? Do you mean when I was confirmed?"

Sally sat back and leaned against the cold prison wall.

"No, Nita. I mean when you . . ." She paused significantly. "Nita, are you saying that you have never asked Jesus Christ to be your personal Saviour?"

"Well, yes, I think so. I learned the doctrines of the church and memorized many of the psalms and hymns when I was young, but—"

"But that isn't the same as being saved, Nita."

"It isn't?"

"No, being saved means that you confess your sin to the Lord and ask Him to make you His child. Have you ever done that?"

"No, I do not think so; not like you say."

"You mean, you—you're not a Christian?" Roy asked in surprise.

"I thought I was."

"But you don't know?" asked Sally. "You don't know for sure?"

Nita spoke with great hesitancy: "No, not ex-

56

actly. I was confirmed when I was 12 years old, and I thought I became a Christian then."

"Nita, being confirmed is fine and even going to church is good," Roy said, "but none of those things make you a child of God."

"You are saying that I do not belong to God?"

"Not me, Nita; the Bible says it."

"But my parents taught me all about God, and I have been faithful to my church and—"

"Nita, listen to what the Bible says."

Roy wished he had his Bible so he could show Nita the verses, but instead he quoted them to her: "'All have sinned, and come short of the glory of God.' 'There is none righteous, no, not one.'"

"No one?" Nita asked in disbelief.

"No one; not even one person. Not you, not me, not Sally."

"I am so mixed up with all this. Oh, Sally, how's your arm?"

"My arm still hurts a little, but Nita, we're talking about something that is more important than my arm. You have to face the question. Are you a Christian?"

"Well, I have never done anything very wrong. I do not steal or swear or hate or do any of those awful things."

"Oh, please, Nita, listen," Sally said tenderly. "I know you're a good person—as good as a sinner can be."

"A sinner?"

"Yes, the Bible says we are all sinners and only when Jesus Christ is our Saviour can our sin be washed away."

"But my church did not teach like that."

"But the Bible does," Roy pointed out.

"Have you ever sinned, Nita?" Sally continued to press the issue.

"Of course; hasn't everyone?"

"That's it exactly. The Bible says everyone has sinned. But the Bible also says that Jesus came to take away that sin—to make you perfect in His sight."

"How do I do that?"

Roy took over again. "First you have to be sincere; you have to mean it. You can't just agree to it because Sally and I are talking to you."

"And if I really mean it, then I am a Christian?"

"Yes, if you confess your sin and trust Jesus to forgive you. Let me give you a verse that my dad gave me when he led me to the Lord. It's John 3:16."

"Oh, I know that verse. I even learned a song about that."

"OK, maybe all three of us should say it together."

"'For God so loved the world, that he gave his only begotten Son, that whosoever believeth in him should not perish, but have everlasting life.'"

"And I do believe that Jesus died for the world," Nita said.

"But do you believe that Jesus died for you?" Roy asked.

Nita was quiet for a long time. When she spoke, she did it softly and meaningfully. "Yes, I do believe."

"And do you believe that He will forgive your sin—when you ask Him?" Sally pressed.

"Yes, I do believe that," Nita confessed.

58

Suddenly the dark, dingy prison in the old Army academy seemed to reflect a new light. It wasn't an electric bulb for everyone to see, but it was there. Even Sally, who only minutes earlier had voiced her dislike for the old building, suddenly found herself enjoying the surroundings. God was there. That was for sure.

"Why don't you pray and tell God about this, Nita?" Roy continued, carefully choosing his words.

"Right here? Do I not need to be in a church?"

"No, Nita, God is right here in this prison," Sally assured her.

"Will you help me? To pray, I mean?"

"Sure, Nita. Just tell Him that you recognize that you're a sinner and that you want Him to forgive your sins and make you His child."

Together the three imprisoned young teens knelt on the cold concrete floor and Nita began to pray. It was a simple prayer, but one of confession and thanksgiving. The place seemed so sacred they almost forgot that they were still trapped.

Roy closed the prayertime, thanking God for the salvation that Nita had just found: "And so, Lord, I even want to thank You for letting us get stuck in here so Nita could find You. Now I pray that You'll send us some help and —" He stopped suddenly.

"What was that?"

"Yes, I heard some rustling of leaves or something," Nita said.

Sally agreed. "And I thought I heard someone move our bicycles."

"Hey out there," Roy called, not even

remembering that he had not finished his prayer. "We're down here."

"We're trapped." Sally joined him and so did Nita.

"Please," Roy repeated. "Down here—in the prison part."

After several minutes of calling they stopped.

"We're rescued," Nita said jubilantly. "I hear footsteps."

They waited quietly, but no one appeared in the prison.

"But I heard footsteps," Nita argued with no one in particular. "I know I did."

"And I was sure I heard our bikes topple over or something," Sally added.

"There's someone out there all right. We just have to get their attention," said Roy. "Down here," he called out again.

"In the basement," Sally called as loudly as she could.

"Why do they not answer?" Nita asked.

"Maybe there's no one out there after all," Sally said. "It wasn't our imaginations, was it?"

"No, I know I heard footsteps," Roy said with firmness. "I know I did."

"But you do not hear anything now, do you?" Nita asked doubtfully.

He gave the signal for silence once again.

"Yes, I do; I do."

They all heard it—a definite rhythmic pattern of someone coming down the long hallway. In spite of the darkness, the three were all able to see the approaching figure. And then, as though to confirm what they saw, there was a loud bark.

"A dog," Roy said, almost disappointed enough to cry. "It's just a dog."

Chapter 8

The Police Officer's Questions

A police car was parked outside the Benton home. Inside, an officer poured another cup of black coffee for Barbara Benton.

"Do you feel any better?" he asked sincerely.

Barbara set the cup down on the table. Her hands were still shaking uncontrollably. "Yes, yes. And don't make me drink any more of this stuff," she said, pointing to the cup. "I'm all right."

"Then maybe you can start giving me a few answers to my questions," he said, taking a small black notebook from his inside coat pocket.

"I'll answer anything," she replied softly. "What do you want to know?"

"Your call," he stated simply. "You reported that both your child and your husband had disappeared. Do you remember that?"

Barbara became a bit irritated. "Of course, I remember. That's why I called," she said indignantly.

"Now, first, about your little girl—how old is she?"

"Little girl?" Barbara repeated loudly. "Sally's in high school."

If the officer was surprised, he didn't show it. "I thought you reported a missing baby."

"Sally is my baby," Barbara stated firmly. "And that husband of mine knows where she is; I'm sure he does."

"What makes you think so?" the officer probed.

"Because he took that call from the camp people."

"Camp people?" the officer repeated. "All right, let's talk about the camp."

"I don't know anything about either the camp or those people," Barbara stated.

"But you say a call came from them?"

"Yes, but Steve wouldn't tell me what it was all about," she said, "except that Sally hadn't shown up."

"And what is the name of the camp?" he asked.

"Oh, I don't know." Barbara shook her head vigorously and then put her hand to her forehead. "Oh, I've got a headache," she grumbled.

"Yes, I'm sure you have," said the police officer. "Now, back to the questions. Tell me anything you know about the camp plans your daughter had."

Barbara Benton told him that Sally had been going to church for some time and that the youth group had planned a weekend bicycle retreat. Then she described how she and Steve had quarreled over Sally's going with the group.

"Do you and your husband fight often?" he asked.

Barbara nodded. "Usually over my drinking," she admitted. "More in the last few days since I wrecked the car."

"The car?" the policeman asked. "The one in the driveway?"

Barbara nodded again.

"I took it to the store the other day," she

paused and carefully chose her words. "I guess I had been drinking a little and . . ." She stopped again, waiting for the officer to inject a question. When he didn't, she continued. "I guess I banged up the fender pretty bad, and that made Steve mad—really mad."

"Banged up the fender?" the officer asked seriously. "I looked that car over before I came in; I didn't see any damage."

Barbara laughed loudly. "Well, if you didn't see that dented left fender and the hole in the garage door, then you shouldn't be a policeman."

"Oh, yes, I saw the damage to the garage, but the car—well, there's nothing wrong with it. It's in beautiful shape."

Barbara stood for the first time since the officer had arrived. "You just come with me," she said, leading the officer through the back door. "I'll show you what I did."

She stopped suddenly in front of the parked car. "That's not our car," she said, surprise in her voice.

"Not your car? Whose is it?" he asked.

"I have no idea," Barbara replied. "Our car is red; this one's blue."

The officer walked all around the car, pulled out his black book and listed the license number in it. Then turning to Barbara, he said, "Could I use your telephone?"

She signaled toward the door.

"I'll call headquarters, and we'll find out whose car this is," he said. "That is if you're sure it isn't yours."

"Of course I'm sure," she said indignantly. "I ought to know our own car." She led the policeman back into the kitchen and pointed to the white telephone sitting on a small table near the window. He dialed headquarters and waited for the station to answer. As he did, Barbara walked slowly into the front part of the house. She could hear him ask for information about the car, giving the make, the year and the license number. She vaguely remembered having seen that car someplace, but for the life of her she couldn't remember where or when.

The officer finished his call and came into the living room. "They'll be calling back shortly," he said. "Can I ask you another question?"

"You can ask as many as you like if you just find my Sally," she said soberly. "That's all I want—Sally."

"Well, there was a number on the telephone pad. I called the operator to see who it belonged to and found it's a Robert Tyler. Do you know anyone by that name?"

Before Barbara could reply the telephone rang, and the officer went to answer it. "That should be information on the car," he said.

Barbara followed him back into the kitchen.

"Tyler?" the officer questioned. "Robert Tyler? Thank you."

He hung up the phone and turned to face Barbara. "Mrs. Benton," he said. "That car belongs to a Robert Tyler, and the number on this telephone pad is also Robert Tyler's. What can you tell me about him?"

Barbara shook her head. "I don't know anyone by that—" she stopped suddenly, searching her mind for more details. She did remember that name. "That's who Steve called to help him find Sally," she announced.

"Is he a friend of your husband's?"

"No," she shook her head, "not really; he goes to the same church that Sally goes to and—"

The officer interrupted. "Can you remember the name of the church yet?"

Barbara continued to shake her head. "No, but it's not far from here; I know that. Sally walks over there every Sunday."

"Well, that helps. There are only a couple of churches within walking distance of this home," he said. "I'll check them out."

Barbara hardly heard him. "You don't think something's happened to her, like . . ." she couldn't finish.

The officer put his hand on Mrs. Benton's shoulder. "No, Ma'am," he said softly. "We had had no accidents, no deaths and no serious injuries reported when I came to your home this afternoon. I think she must be all right."

He put his book, along with a picture of Sally, into his pocket. He looked at the distraught lady. "Will you be all right now?" he asked.

"All right?" Barbara said softly. "No, I won't be all right until Sally is back in this house."

"Yes, I can understand how you feel, and I'll get someone on the case right away," he said matter-of-factly. "And if I were you, I'd lay off the bottle. That won't help either you or your daughter."

Barbara looked straight up at him, tears in her eyes. "Sir, I'm not going to drink," she said firmly. "In fact, if you find my Sally, I'll never take another drink as long as I live. I promise."

67

"That sounds good, Mrs. Benton," said the officer, "but it usually takes more than a promise to change a habit like yours."

Barbara refused to agree with him. "You just find my Sally," she repeated, "and I'll show you that I can give it up."

Then she burst into tears and fled from the room.

The officer watched her leave, and then he let himself out the front door. Sitting in the cruiser, he filled out the forms for the missing persons' report. He shook his head as he wrote. Why did people drink? Why did they let a substance in a bottle control their lives? Why?

Chapter 9

Nice Dog

Even in the darkness of the old prison, Roy could see the form of a dog. For a moment he became angry. Why had God sent only a dog when He knew they needed a person to get them out of here?

"Just a dog," he repeated. "Just somebody's pet dog."

The others shared his disappointment. But suddenly Sally brightened.

"Hey," she said, getting the attention of her friends. "That's it; he's somebody's pet."

"So?" Roy said, still disgusted. "A lot of good that'll do us."

"I do not understand why you are getting all excited about a pet," Nita said, sharing Roy's lack of enthusiasm.

"Don't you see?" she continued excitedly. "If he's someone's pet, then there must be someone around here. He wouldn't be way out here alone."

"Hey," Roy brightened noticeably. "Maybe you're right."

"But who does he belong to?" Nita asked, still wondering how a dog could help them.

"I don't know," Roy stated. "But probably whoever owns that garden we saw near the road."

"Garden! What garden?" Sally wanted to know.

"Didn't you see it?" Roy asked. "There was a

69

big garden plot just about where we left the road and made our own path."

"If you say there was a garden there, then there must be a garden there," Nita agreed. "I guess I was so worried about not seeing a path, I did not look around for anything else."

Roy had another thought. "Now we'll have to figure out how we can get the guy's attention; you know, let him know we're down here."

"Well, if we tie a white handkerchief or something on the dog's collar and send him out, his owner will see that it's a distress signal and —" Sally stopped. "But no one has a handkerchief?" she said, making the question sound like a statement of fact.

"Not me," Roy confessed.

"I have one—in my backpack out with my bike," Nita added, discouragement showing in her voice.

"And we don't have any pencils or paper either, do we?" Roy added, squelching Sally's idea for a distress signal.

"Oh, well," Sally managed. "It was a good thought anyway."

Roy sighed deeply. "Yeah, I thought for a minute that the Lord had given us an idea for a way out."

"Maybe He has," Nita said brightly. "That is if Sally will agree to it."

"Agree to it? Just tell me what to do. I want to get out of here, too, remember?"

"What are you thinking, Nita?" Roy pressed.

"Well, that handkerchief idea made me think of it," Nita replied.

"Come on, Nita; forget the details. Just tell us

70

your idea." Sally's impatience was beginning to show.

"Your necklace," Nita stated simply.

"My necklace?" Sally said, tugging at the chain around her neck.

"Yes," Nita said. "It has your name on it, right?"

"Yeah, Dad had it engraved when he gave it to me for Christmas."

"I must be stupid," Roy said. "I still don't get it."

"Oh, I do," Sally exclaimed. "We can hook this necklace on the dog's collar and then send him back to his owner."

"And then when the gardener sees it, he will know that someone by the name of Sally is in trouble someplace," Nita finished.

"But how will he know where we are?" Sally asked, not sure that Nita's idea was such a good one after all.

"That's a chance we'll have to take," Roy said getting up from the floor. "Nita, you help Sally with the necklace, and I'll get Rover to come a little closer to this gate."

"Rover?" Sally said, laughing. "I'll bet that's not his name."

"OK then," Roy continued, "Fido."

Laughter rang out through the cold prison cell for the first time in many minutes.

"Come on, whatever your name is," Roy called. "Come on over here, Shep."

Nita pushed aside Sally's long hair and unclasped the necklace. Then she joined Roy in calling the dog.

"Here doggie. Here," she said, her accent still amusing the others.

"What do you suppose his name really is?" Sally asked, helping the others lure the dog closer so they could reach him.

"I don't know; maybe Spot," Roy said, laughing. "Except there's not really a spot of any kind on him."

"Buster?" Sally asked.

"Buster?" Roy laughed loudly. "Who'd ever name a dog 'Buster'?"

"Here dog, come on dog," Roy continued, extending his arm through the bars of the iron gate.

"Here, nice doggie," Nita said softly, and with that the large German shepherd walked slowly toward the gate.

"That must be his name," Sally laughed. "Nice Dog."

Roy held on to the collar, and with Nita's help they fastened Sally's necklace securely to it.

"Now, scram, beat it," Roy said, giving the dog a gentle push.

But the big dog only looked at him through the bars.

"Aw, come on, Nice Dog. Scram. Go back to your master," Roy continued.

Sally shook her head slightly, pushing her hair away from her face.

"I'll bet he wonders why we call him to come to us one minute and then try to make him get out of here the next minute."

Nita agreed. "That does not make sense, does it?"

"You're right. He doesn't understand our

plans at all," Roy said, still trying to give the dog a push toward the big corridor.

"Boy, that's sure a good illustration for a Christian." Sally's note of seriousness got the attention of Nita and Roy.

"What do you mean?" Nita asked.

"Well, that poor dog thought we were his friends. Then all of a sudden we seem like enemies, pushing him out."

"Hey, I get it," Roy said cheerfully. "Sometimes we think God is helping us, and then when something goes differently than the way we had planned, we think God isn't treating us right. So we rebel."

Sally nodded. "Yes, and all the time He has some bigger and better things for us—something we didn't see at the time."

"Oh, that is a beautiful thought," Nita said. She reached out to the dog, petted him tenderly and spoke in soft tones.

"Now doggie, you can rescue us if you will just do what we ask."

The big dog looked into the face of the German girl as though he understood.

"Now, you turn around and go up that corridor," she said, pointing. "And go back to your master. Please?"

Sally and Roy watched in amazement. As though on signal the large dog did exactly as Nita had commanded. He turned slowly, and then he began walking down the long corridor. Everyone listened as he went up the concrete steps and out of the building.

"He did it," Roy screamed. "He did it."

"Terrific," Sally added, a thrill in her voice.

73

"Now we'd better pray that he goes straight back to his master."

"And that his master sees your necklace," Nita said, a bit of concern in her voice.

"And that it all makes sense to him," Roy finished.

"I agree. Let's pray about it."

Sitting down on the cold floor, the three had another prayertime. Nita started with a short to-the-point prayer, asking God to let the owner of the dog find the necklace and sense the need that it represented. Sally thanked the Lord for the Christmas present her dad had given her and asked Him to use it to bring about their release from the old building. Just before she closed, she even asked God to keep the rats away and to help everyone maintain a cheerful attitude. Roy closed the prayertime, thanking the Lord for the lessons they were learning and asking forgiveness for not believing that God could use the dog. He thanked the Lord for doing things His way instead of their way. A soft amen was uttered from the lips of each of them as they closed their time of prayer and thanksgiving.

"We are praying like this has already worked," Nita said, a touch of doubt in her voice.

"That's because we believe God is going to answer," Roy assured her.

"But how can you know for sure?" she insisted.

"That's faith, Nita," Roy said briefly. "The Christian life is a life of faith. And the Bible says when we ask something in God's name, that He'll answer. He'll do it."

"Oh, my," she said, thinking about Roy's ex-

74

planation. "I have many things to learn, do I not?"

"We all have, Nita," Sally said quickly. "I don't think we ever learn everything. I've even heard Pastor Don say that he learns new things about the Christian life all the time."

The mention of Pastor Don's name brought their thoughts back to the weekend retreat—something they had almost forgotten.

"Wonder what they're doing there now?" Roy mused.

"I'll bet they're praying," Sally offered.

"Just think," Nita said, thinking aloud. "They asked me to give my testimony tonight." She paused thoughtfully. "I wonder what I would have said since I did not really belong to Jesus until now?"

Roy shifted his position and quietly quoted a line his father had used many times: " 'God works in mysterious ways, His wonders to perform.'" Then after a short, thoughtful pause, he spoke again with a note of joy in his voice: "Hey! You know what I think we ought to do?"

The girls answered in unison, "What?"

"Sing," Roy said simply.

"Sing?" Nita asked. "Here?"

"Yeah, that's what Paul and Silas did. Remember the lesson we were talking about? They sang, so why can't we?"

Sally agreed.

"OK," Roy said, standing and mocking his father's morning service motions. "Let's all turn to hymn number 4000."

"Four thousand?" Nita said, not sure if Roy was serious or joking.

"OK, would you rather sing 3000?" he asked, a smile toying on the corners of his lips.

"Yeah," Sally remarked. "I think I like that one better."

Roy laughed out loud. "OK, now if one of you will just tell me what that song is, we'll be all set."

The spirit in the old prison brightened as the three began to sing some of the songs they had learned in church and Sunday school. Nita did not know all of them, and Sally and Roy could not remember all of the words, but there was a spirit of happiness and praise in the old prison that none of them could deny. It was the kind of experience that only a true child of God could understand. Their voices echoed throughout the corridors of the old deserted Army academy building.

Chapter 10

More Searching

Karen Tyler continued her trek through the high weeds and wooded areas. Even when the others had given up, feeling it was time to report back to camp, Karen had insisted on continuing to search. She was concerned about Roy and Sally, but she knew in her heart that she was really making a desperate search for Nita.

All her terrible thoughts and actions toward the German girl loomed before her. And while the thoughts plagued her, they also spurred her on in her continued search.

Karen was a Christian; she had been brought up in a Christian home and had trusted Christ. But she knew she had not been kind to Nita. Many times she had read the verses in the Bible that told her to be kind, tenderhearted and forgiving. But she had been just the opposite.

She thought Nita was a Christian, too, but she couldn't be sure. The one time she had asked about her spiritual life, Nita had become quite angry. And Karen couldn't blame her. After all, who had she thought she was to probe into another person's spiritual stand when she had showed anything but Christian love to the lonely girl?

Karen remembered when Nita first came and how glad she had been that her parents had taken the stranger in. But then things changed, and Nita had suddenly become a threat to her, a wedge between Karen and her folks. Or so it had seemed anyway.

"I'm sorry, Lord," she whispered. "Really sorry."

Quickly she wiped a falling tear from her eye. "If you'll let me find her, I'll confess everything to her and tell her how wrong I've been. Please, Lord?"

Karen realized she was walking over the same area she had walked through only an hour ago. Lunchtime had come and gone long ago, and she had hardly noticed the empty feeling in her stomach. Right now, she had to find Nita. That was all there was to it. She had to be sure the girl was safe and unharmed. But more than that, she had to get things straightened out with her, something she should have done long ago.

A large German shepherd dog ran past her, stopped suddenly and then returned to where Karen was standing. He barked loudly, as if to call for attention. Karen petted him absent-mindedly. Ordinarily she would have picked up a stick and thrown it to see if he would fetch and return it. But right now there was only one thing on her mind—Nita. She just wasn't in the mood for playing with someone's dog. Then she noticed the chain dangling from the dog's collar.

"Hey, that's Sally's necklace," she said aloud. "Where'd you get this, doggie?"

But before she could unclasp the necklace, the big dog ran into the high weeds and disappeared from view.

"Here, dog, come here, dog," she called. But she knew it was too late. He had made a quick turn and was completely out of sight. For an instant she thought she should follow him. But that was useless, she told herself. It would probably be better to go in the direction from which he had come. Nita and Roy and Sally were probably hurt someplace over there. That chain around the dog's neck had to mean that he had been where they were, that was for sure.

Suddenly Karen was ashamed of herself. She had spent so much time wondering about the dog—who he belonged to, where he had been and where he was headed—that she hadn't even thanked the Lord for this ray of hope that He had sent. She stopped momentarily in the tall grass, asked God to guide her to the place where the dog had been and thanked Him sincerely for sending the big animal her way. When she had finished, she began walking with determination, constantly calling, "Nita, Nita."

* * *

Some distance away, Steve Benton and Bob Tyler sat in the car looking at the "Road Closed" sign.

Steve was angry; that was evident from the sound of his voice.

"For crying out loud," he said, swearing again. "Bridge Washed Out."

"Sure is," Tyler responded, looking beyond the sign.

"Well, that's not going to stop me," Steve announced. "I'm going to get to the academy if it's the last thing I do."

"And it probably will be," Bob Tyler answered, pointing to an old bridge just a few hundred feet beyond the sign. "That bridge really is out."

79

Steve Benton swore angrily and then backed the car onto the main road. For a minute or two he sat there, letting the motor idle and staring at the blocked road.

"A lot of good all your praying did," he snapped.

"I think it did, Steve," Bob Tyler replied calmly.

Steve turned to stare at his passenger.

"I sure don't see how you figure that. We haven't found Sally."

"But we found Karen," he offered. "And it was through her that you were reminded of the old academy."

"But we can't get there," he shouted. "And we don't even know that the kids are there anyway."

That was the first time Steve Benton had acknowledged that there were other young people besides his daughter involved. Bob Tyler noticed it but decided to say nothing about it.

"Well, there's one thing sure," he said instead. "We can't just sit here. If there isn't another road around here, we'd better go back the way we came."

Steve swore again, then put the car in gear and drove in silence for several minutes. Finally he spoke.

"Well, I can tell you one thing," he said as he tromped on the gas pedal. "You won't have to look for me at church Sunday."

"Backing out already?" Bob responded kindly.

"Backing out?" Steve snapped. "God didn't keep His part of the bargain, so why should I keep mine?"

Bob Tyler smiled faintly.

"Steve, I'd love to see you in church this Sunday; I really would. But it's like I told you—God doesn't make bargains with people. Salvation is free. True, it cost God His only begotten Son, but to us it's free. All we have to do is —"

"Knock it off, will you, Tyler? I've had just about all I can take for one day," he exclaimed. "This whole thing with Sally—it's my fault," he went on, anguish in his voice.

"Your fault? How's that?" Bob Tyler asked with genuine concern and tenderness.

"Well, Sally wasn't going on this retreat. Barbara had begged her to stay home with her. And when I heard that, it made me mad." He paused, groping for the right words. "I wasn't going to let Barbara's drinking take any more fun out of Sally's life. It's been hard on the kid, and this was the last straw."

"So you encouraged her to go?"

"Encouraged her? I practically forced her to leave the house!"

Steve slowed down as they reached a curve in the road.

"I told myself that I wanted Sally to have fun and to be with the kids and—well, all kinds of things like that."

"But that doesn't mean you're to blame for her being lost."

"But that wasn't my reason at all," Steve continued, hardly hearing Bob's words. "I just wanted to prove to Barbara that I was the big shot in our house. What I said had to go."

"And now Barbara's angry with you because Sally's missing?"

"Angry? She's furious. And I can't really blame her. She told me it was all my fault for forcing Sally out of the house and . . ."

Steve stopped long enough to get his composure.

"Bob, if I don't find my girl, I'll never be able to live with myself. It's my fault, and both Barbara and I know it."

"And you feel God is punishing you for the rash decision you made?"

Steve's answer was soft-spoken. "Sure looks that way, doesn't it?"

Bob Tyler turned to face the distraught man.

"Well, it's true that God often uses circumstances to get to us. And maybe He is allowing this so He can get you to see yourself as you really are—a sinner."

Steve's expression changed noticeably.

"That's a low blow, Tyler. I feel rotten about it, sure. But I don't know how you think you've got the right to tell a guy he's a sinner."

"From the Bible, Steve. That's where I found out that I was one."

Steve's lips tightened.

"Well, let me tell you something, Mr. Christian. If it weren't for me, our home would have broken up years ago, I can tell you that much. My wife is sure a sinner, if there ever was one."

"And you're not?" Tyler asked, kindness still strong in his voice.

"She drinks; I don't—at least I don't get drunk. She makes more problems than Sally and me put together. She uses our money for booze and . . ."

"And that makes her bad and you good. Right?"

"OK, that's enough. If I'd known you were going to pound all this religion into me, I wouldn't have called you."

"And why did you call me, Steve?"

Steve Benton did not answer. Clutching the steering wheel firmly, he pondered his friend's words. Deep in his heart he knew why he had called Karen's father—Bob was a praying man, a Christian. But somehow, he could not bring himself to tell his companion the truth.

Chapter 11

"We're Rescued!"

Steve Benton was not familiar with gravel-road driving, and it showed in the way he controlled the car. But he was determined to keep going without reducing his speed. If Sally and the others were hurt or sick, time could be vitally important.

Bob Tyler was also concerned about the safety of the young people. But he was even more concerned about Steve's driving. With one eye he scanned the area for any sight of the missing campers. With the other eye he watched the speedometer.

"I wouldn't take it too fast on this gravel," he warned cautiously. But Steve made no attempt to slow down. As he came around a curve, Bob Tyler sat up with a start.

"Look out! There's a dog!" he called.

Steve swerved the car, missing the big animal by inches. Then he spouted off a stream of swear words.

"Stupid dog," Steve muttered. "You'd think his owner would have kept him closer to home, especially out here in no-man's-land."

Bob Tyler brightened. "Hey, I think you've got a point."

"Of course I've got a point," Steve retorted, not waiting for Bob's explanation.

"No, I don't mean about the owners' keeping

their dog tied up; I mean a dog being way out here where there are no homes."

Steve shrugged. "Well, maybe it's just a stray."

"No, I don't think so," Tyler said more convincingly than before. "That was a mighty beautiful dog; he belongs to someone, I'm sure."

"So?"

"So that means there has to be an owner somewhere around here."

Steve had been somewhat irritated with Bob Tyler for pressing the "religion" issue earlier, but now that was forgotten.

"Hey, I think you're right," he said, finally slowing down the car.

"Let's keep our eyes open for a tent or a cabin or something," Tyler said confidently. "Maybe someone's just out here for the weekend."

"Well, there aren't any houses around here," Steve said. "That's for sure."

Slowly they moved up the gravel road, watching carefully for any signs of activity.

"Hey, there's a garden," Bob Tyler said, pointing to a well-cared-for plot. "And a pickup."

"Well, we're not looking for a garden or a truck," Steve reminded him. "We're looking for people."

"Well, now think about it, Steve; if there's a garden that well cared for, there's got to be a gardener somewhere around here. And that pickup didn't drive itself here."

Reluctantly Steve admitted that his passenger could be right.

"Maybe we'd better stop and take a look around," he said. But before he could bring the car to a halt by the side of the road, the big German shepherd appeared on the road again.

"There's the dog again," Tyler said. "There has to be someone nearby."

Steve brought the car to a stop and opened the door on his side.

"Maybe we can get him to lead us to his owner," he said, sounding more encouraged than he had before.

"Here, dog," Tyler called, patting his leg. The big animal obeyed immediately. Bob petted the dog for a brief moment and then called to Steve.

"Look," he said, a question in his voice. He held a necklace dangling from the dog's collar and read the inscription aloud. "'Sally from Dad.'"

"What?" Steve shouted, kneeling down beside the dog and Bob.

"'Sally from Dad,'" Bob Tyler read again.

"That's Sally's necklace!" Steve shouted. "It's the one I gave her for Christmas!"

"You sure?" Bob asked, not really meaning to question his companion.

Steve's temper rose again.

"Of course, I'm sure. I ought to know what I gave my daughter for Christmas."

"Then this dog has been where the kids are," Tyler said confidently.

As they talked, a man walked toward them from the garden area.

"You like my dog?" he asked, still holding an old hoe in his hand.

"Hi there," Bob said in a friendly voice. "Yes, we were admiring your dog, all right."

"Where's he been?" Steve asked abruptly.

"Manchester? Oh, I don't know," the man

87

drawled. "He runs around all over the place while I'm working in the garden."

Bob Tyler introduced himself and his companion.

"And my name's Pete Chandler," the man said, shaking hands with each of them.

"What brings you out this way?"

Steve seemed not to hear his question.

"You don't know where your dog has been?" he asked again.

"Well, no, not really. He runs around and discovers all kinds of things, I guess."

"Like where?" Steve insisted.

"Oh, more than once I've found him down by that old Army academy building."

"Where is that building?" Steve asked impatiently.

"Down a ways through the tall weeds," he said. "You ain't planning to go down there, are you?"

"Yes," Steve replied quickly. "We need to get to that academy. Can you take us there?"

Pete Chandler hesitated, looking back at his garden work.

"Well," he said slowly. "Sure, I s'pose I could after I get things done here. But I might just as well tell you, there ain't nothing there to see."

"We think there might be some young people there," Bob said, feeling he should explain. "And we're concerned about their welfare."

"My daughter's with them," Steve added quickly. "She could be hurt or sick."

"And we think your dog was there with her," Bob finished.

"Oh?" Pete questioned simply. "And what makes you think Manchester's been with them?"

"This necklace," Bob said, stooping down to show Pete Chandler the necklace on the dog's collar.

Pete looked at the chain, unclasped it from the collar and read the inscription. "And Sally's your daughter?" he asked, pointing to the frustrated man at his side.

Steve nodded but did not speak. Right at that moment he was more concerned about Sally than he'd ever been in his life. The very fact that Sally would sacrifice her treasured necklace to get the attention of the dog's owner had to mean that she was in terrible danger.

"If you'll give me a minute, I'll go to my truck and get some tools," Pete said, recognizing the problem as a serious one.

"I don't think we'll need tools," Steve barked. "Just take us to this building."

"Well, OK. But we'll have to walk. Not even my old pickup can plow through the weeds and brush that have grown over the path. Manchester can probably lead the way though."

With that he knelt down beside the dog again and put his arm around the furry animal.

"Now, Manchester, you take us to that building you were at today. You understand? It's very important."

For a brief second Steve bristled at the tactics the man was using, but since he had no better ideas, he remained silent.

"Go, Manchester. Now go," Pete called.

The big dog seemed to understand the urgency he had helped to create and began to run through

89

the high weeds in the direction from which he had come.

"Seems to know what you want all right," Bob said, running along with the others.

"Oh, that Manchester is one smart dog. You talk to him like you do to a person," Pete said.

"Well, I hope he gets us there in time," Steve said, struggling to keep up with the big dog.

"Guess we're not in as good a shape as your dog is," Bob said, breathing heavily.

Pete Chandler called his dog back.

"Here, Manchester. Come back here, boy."

The dog obeyed the orders and returned to the spot where the three men had stopped for a brief rest.

"We can't lose him," Pete stated frankly. "With the weeds as high as they are this time of year, it's easy to get confused and head in the wrong direction without realizing it."

Pete Chandler bent down and talked to his dog again. "You wait for us," he said simply. Then giving the dog a pat, he sent him on the way again.

"I think your dog senses a problem," Bob Tyler said, walking with the gardener.

"Oh, sure he does," Pete answered. "He's one smart dog, I'll say that."

"Did you train him?" Steve asked, showing an interest in something other than his daughter for a moment.

"Nope. A missionary gave him to us," Pete said. "All trained and beautiful."

"A missionary?" Bob's interest showed in his voice.

"That's right. He was owned by a missionary

family home on furlough. When they went back to the field, they asked us if we wanted their dog."

"Are you a-a-Christian?" Bob asked hesitantly.

"A Christian? Sure am," Pete said. "Accepted the Lord many years ago. You men know the Lord, do you?"

Steve Benton changed the subject abruptly. "Shouldn't we be there pretty soon?"

"Can't be too much farther," Pete answered.

At that moment a voice echoed in the distance.

"What was that?" Steve asked.

Pete Chandler stopped and looked around. "I thought I heard a girl's voice."

"I did too," Bob answered. "Sounded like she was calling for someone."

"We must be close to where Sally is," Steve said. "Where's the dog?"

"Here, Manchester," Pete called.

At that moment the girl's voice came through more clearly.

"Nita!" Karen Tyler called loudly. "Nita, where are you?"

"That's Karen," Bob said.

"Karen one of the missing ones?" Pete asked with interest.

"No, she's *my* daughter," Bob Tyler replied.

"Well, the plot thickens," Pete said, laughing ever so slightly.

"What we don't need is some bad jokes," Steve said irritably. "This is no time for joking."

Pete Chandler apologized. "I'm sorry," he said. "I'm just a bit mixed up on who we're looking for and why they'd come here in the first place."

Bob explained briefly what had happened. As

91

he did, the men could hear Karen's voice. This time it was closer.

"Oh, you came back," she said, talking to the German shepherd. "Show me where they are."

The big dog barked as if to reply.

"Karen," Bob called out. "Wait for us."

"Dad, I think this dog knows where they are."

"Yes, we think so too. He led us here."

"Well, I saw him before. And when I spotted Sally's necklace hanging on his neck, I figured they had to be someplace in the direction he had come from. There's an old building right over there. I think it's the old academy building. Maybe that's where they are."

"Good thinking, young lady," Pete said, smiling broadly at the girl.

Suddenly everyone stopped talking.

"Singing. I hear singing," Bob said enthusiastically.

"I do too," Karen agreed. "It's them; they're singing church songs."

"I don't know how they can be singing when they're lost," Steve ventured.

As he spoke they saw the three bicycles.

"Dad, the bikes," Karen called out.

By this time they could hear the words of the song clearly:

"Trust and obey—For there's no other way
To be happy in Jesus But to trust and
    obey."

"Nita!" Karen called loudly in spite of her weariness.

Down in the old prison Nita stopped singing. "Someone is calling my name," she said, shock in her voice.

"Yeah, I heard it too," Roy admitted.

For a moment he thought they must have been dreaming. But then another voice rang out loud and clear.

"Sally! Oh, Sally."

"That's my dad's voice," Sally said excitedly. "We're rescued! We're rescued!"

Chapter 12

Whose Fault?

The three young people stood up in excitement. They had prayed that God would send someone to rescue them, but they had hardly dared to believe as firmly as they should have. And when the big dog had visited them, they had almost expressed disappointment rather than hope. But now they could hear the voices of people, and they knew they had been found.

"We're downstairs," Roy called loudly. "Down in the prison part."

As he called he heard the patter of light footsteps again. And suddenly the same German shepherd dog appeared beside the gate. For a moment, the three teens were stunned.

"It's the dog again," Sally said, disappointment evident in her voice.

"No, it cannot be," Nita said with emphasis. "I heard my name."

Roy stroked the dog affectionately. "Hey, your necklace is gone. He took the message to someone."

He cupped his hands to his mouth again. "Down here," he called over and over again, making sure whoever was outside would come all the way down into the cold, dark basement area.

"We're trapped down here," Sally chimed in to be sure her father would hear and recognize her voice.

In a moment there were more footsteps. Someone was running frantically down the long corridor.

"Karen!" Nita called in surprise. "What are you doing here?"

"We found you; we found you!" Karen cried, tears coursing down her cheeks.

Soon the old prison area seemed to be filled with people. And everyone was talking at once. Even Manchester was barking.

"Sally?" Steve Benton asked. "You all right?"

Questions and answers flowed so freely that no one seemed to realize the three young people had not yet left the prison.

"Well, now, you ain't gonna stay in there, are you?" Pete Chandler asked finally.

Roy gave the gate a shake.

"We are unless someone can get us out," Roy answered. "We're trapped in here."

"Trapped?" Steve said, shaking the old gate just as Roy had done. "You've got to be kidding."

"I wish we were," Roy said, speaking for the girls as well as himself.

"Well, what happened?" Steve barked. "Why can't you get out of there?"

"Something broke, Dad," Sally explained. "We've tried to budge that gate about a hundred times."

"I knew I should have brought my tools," Pete remarked, looking over at Steve. "I just had the feeling we'd need them."

"Well, how'd you get stuck in here in the first place?" Steve blurted angrily. "And what made you come to this stupid building when you were supposed to go to that camp?" He fired one question after another, not allowing anyone time to answer or explain.

When he finally stopped, Roy cleared his throat nervously. He had known all along that eventually he would have to explain everything, and it looked like this was the dreaded moment.

"Well, Mr. Benton," he began. "I guess it's all my fault."

"I might have known," Steve snapped.

Sally took hold of Roy's arm. "It isn't your fault, Roy," she managed.

"Well, I'm the one who picked this place for our singspiration and stuff."

"But we wanted to come here too," Nita defended.

"I thought this would be a good spot to take the retreat group tonight," Roy continued. "I asked Nita and Sally if they'd like to go and see it while I checked it out."

"You brought these girls here?" Steve said, raising his voice angrily. "You're the one who did this?"

"I'm sorry, really I am," Roy managed.

"Well, you ought to be. I don't know what kind of a church group you're with, but I can tell you this much, they're going to hear from me about all this."

Bob Tyler decided he had listened as long as he should without getting in on the conversation. Finally, he spoke. "Now, Steve, let's not dwell on the problem; let's just thank the Lord that the kids are all right and that we've found them."

"Amen," said Pete Chandler. With that he gave the old gate another shake. "Can't figure out how this thing got locked like this. Every time I

97

was down here, you could open and close it without any trouble."

"I'm to blame for that," Sally confessed.

"You?" questioned her father.

"No, it is not your fault alone," Nita defended again.

Steve Benton's temper came to the surface again.

"Would you people stop trying to defend each other and just explain what happened?"

Roy began to tell how they had explored the upstairs area and were about to leave when he told the girls he used to come here as a child.

"So I challenged him to chin himself on this gate," Sally confessed, after Roy had explained his childhood defeat.

"So?" Steve asked wondering what that had to do with everything that had taken place.

"Well, a rat started crawling around and headed right toward Sally."

"And you know how scared I am of bugs and things," she added quickly.

"How could the rat make the gate lock?" Karen asked, and then realized how silly her question sounded.

"I was trying to dodge it," Sally said. "And I whammed into this gate pretty hard. When I did, something fell."

"This," Nita said, picking up the rusty piece of metal that was to have held the latch in place.

Pete Chandler took the small piece in his hand.

"Looks like it rusted out," he said. "Yup, this could be the culprit, all right."

"Do you think we can work that gate without it?" questioned Bob Tyler.

"We can sure try," Chandler agreed.

With that Karen and the three men on the outside worked hard to make the old door open, but without success.

"Roy, you pull up on that handle," Bob Tyler said, "while we push out here."

Together they worked it again, but the latch still would not release.

"Well, we'd just as well face it," Pete ventured. "I'd better go back for some tools."

"You can take our bikes," Roy volunteered. "That'll save some time."

"Maybe I'll just do that," Pete grinned.

"I think I'll go along," Tyler said. "We should call the camp and tell them the kids have been found."

"I have a CB in my pickup," Pete announced. "You can get word to the people back home, too, if you want."

"Good," Bob said. Then he turned to Steve and asked, "Want to come along and talk with your wife?"

Steve seemed disinterested. "Naw. I'll wait."

"Dad," Sally said. "You mean Mom knows that we're lost?"

"Well, I think so. You know, you can never tell for sure about your mother."

"But she'll be worried. Shouldn't you call her and tell her we're safe?"

"Sure, come on along, Steve," Pete encouraged.

"I'll stay here with my daughter," he snapped. Then turning to Sally, he said softly, "Your mother

99

is probably bombed again. There's no use calling her."

"But Dad," Sally begged.

"Forget it," Steve replied. "We'll tell her together—when you get home."

"Well, we'd better be on our way," Pete Chandler said. "Or these kids'll be here all night."

"No thanks," Roy said laughing. "Daytime is bad enough. Nighttime would be awful."

Bob Tyler turned to Karen, who had been unusually quiet.

"Honey, you want to come along and let us take you back to camp?"

"No, Dad," Karen said softly. "I need to talk to Nita. And I think I'll stay and do it now."

By this time Steve was getting nervous.

"Well, are you guys going for tools or aren't you?"

"We're on our way," Pete said cheerfully. "Come on, Manchester."

"Manchester!" Roy laughed. "Is that his name?"

"Sure is," Pete said proudly. "Course, I didn't name him, but I think it fits."

"You know what we called him?" Roy asked, laughing loudly. "We called him 'Fido' and 'Rover' and storybook names like that."

Even Steve Benton laughed this time. "You mean you'd call a dog this size 'Fido'?"

For the moment everyone seemed more relaxed than they had been for some time. Laughter filled the old Army academy building, echoing up through the corridors.

"OK, folks, we'll be back as soon as we can. Now don't you run off while we're gone," Pete said,

100

teasing the three who were still very much trapped.

"Believe me," Roy said positively. "If there was any way, we sure would give it a try."

Manchester barked loudly as he ran down the corridor and up the steps to the outside.

"Boy, that is some dog," Roy said. "And do you remember what I said when he came down here the first time?"

Nita nodded. "Oh, yes! I remember you said, 'Just a dog!'"

"Yeah, we had been praying for someone to come and rescue us, and when the dog came, we thought God had forgotten what we needed," Sally finished.

"But God had a reason for allowing all this," Karen finally ventured.

"Oh, yes, that is right," Nita said jubilantly. "And I am the reason."

"No, I think I am," Karen said almost apologetically.

"But no, I must tell you what happened here," Nita injected.

"Yeah, Karen, it was really neat," Roy added. "Well, I should let Nita tell you."

As the others began to talk, Steve Benton edged as close to the gate as he could to talk with his daughter.

"Are you really all right, Sally?" he asked. "You look a little, well, sicklike."

"No, I'm not sick, Dad," Sally replied. "My arm still hurts a little."

"What happened to your arm?"

"I'm not sure, Dad. I saw that rat and got scared. Then I guess I hit the gate with my arm, and then I fainted."

"Fainted?" he questioned. "You've never fainted in your life."

"Well, I have now."

Steve interrupted the others' conversation. "What happened?" he barked, looking first at Roy and then at his daughter.

"I'm not sure. All I know is my arm has been hurting ever since this whole thing happened. I think I just banged it, and maybe I landed wrong when I fell. It's scratched a little too."

Fear came across Steve's face. He turned and looked at Roy again.

"You, whatever your name is—you are going to be in trouble when you get out of here. You mark my words. If my daughter is sick or hurt, you and your stupid church group are going to be hearing from my lawyer. Just you remember that."

"Dad!" Sally cried out. "Dad, it isn't Roy's fault. And it's not Nita's fault."

Steve put his hand on his forehead.

"Not that again."

"Yes," Sally said forcefully. "I'm the one who suggested that we come down here. And I'm the one who got so scared that I ran into the gate and fainted and fell. And if you're going to blame anyone, you'd better blame me. Because I did it."

Steve turned from the gate angrily. He was furious with somebody, but he wasn't sure who. Suddenly he recalled the awful scene that had taken place at home before Sally left. And then he knew who was to blame. It wasn't Roy or the church group; it wasn't even Sally. It was Steve Benton. He had caused it all.

Chapter 13

"Something Happened to Me"

Karen Tyler stood silently looking at her three friends behind the prison bars. She wasn't sure how to start her conversation, but she knew she had to apologize to Nita. Fighting back the tears, Karen extended her arm through the barred prison gate.

"Something happened to me today, Nita," she began softly. "And I want to tell you about it."

"And something happened to me today," Nita said. "And I will tell you about it too."

But before Nita could say anymore, Karen blurted out her own confession.

"I've resented you, Nita. Terribly. And I've resented Mom and Dad for all the nice things they've done for you." She stopped and took a deep breath. Nita opened her mouth to say something, but Karen held her hand up, indicating that she was not through. There was more, lots more, that she had to tell the German girl before she would feel things were right again. Nita understood the signal and said nothing.

"Even today," Karen began again. "Even today when I saw that you got into Roy's and Sally's group, I got angry at you. It wasn't your fault; I knew that. But I was still mad at you."

Roy stepped closer to the gate where Karen and Nita were still holding hands.

"But Karen," he said softly. "You knew we drew names for the groups."

She nodded silently, so he continued.

"I was as surprised as anyone when I saw who was in my group. But it wasn't a put-up job; I can tell you that." He spoke seriously, endeavoring with every word to convince Karen that things had just worked out that way.

"I know," Karen said finally. "I think I knew it then too. But . . ." she stopped, trying to gain her composure. "But I was angry with Nita for—for disrupting our home, I guess. And I wanted to blame her for it."

There, it was out. She had said those dreadful words that had plagued her so much today.

Nita tried again to enter the conversation, but Karen stopped her once more.

"Please, Nita. If I don't say this now, I may chicken out," she said sincerely.

Nita gave Karen's hand an understanding squeeze.

"I need to ask your forgiveness, Nita," she started again. "I have been just awful to you." She paused momentarily. "And I've been an awful Christian too."

Nita could hold back the words no longer.

"Oh, but Karen, it has not been all your fault."

"Well, maybe not, but I just want you to know that today, when I thought something had happened to you, I felt just terrible."

Tears welled up in her eyes as she spoke.

"And Nita. I told the Lord that I was sorry and that I would tell you I was sorry if He would help me find you."

The old prison cell suddenly seemed to take on

a hallowed sense. Neither Sally nor Roy spoke, and Steve Benton stood silently listening to the girl's confession.

Finally Nita broke the silence.

"Karen, you are not to blame for your feelings, at least not all of them. I have been a very resentful person for a long time. I hated all the things that have happened to me—losing my parents, moving to another country and . . ." she stopped.

"And having to live with a person like me," Karen finished for her.

"And I became very bitter. No, I mean angry. And when I saw how you did not like me," she stopped again, swallowed hard and then went on. "I hated you for it. But Karen, I love you now. I really do."

Nita stopped and began to sob uncontrollably. Sally put her arm around the German girl, holding her tightly. When Nita felt she had gained her composure, she began again.

"But today, something happened to me. I trusted Jesus Christ as my personal Saviour. Down here." She pointed to the prison floor.

Karen's eyes brightened. "You—you did?" she asked in surprise.

"Yes," Nita continued. "I had never done that before. I thought I was a Christian because I had gone to church all my life. I had learned the catechism and had sung all the songs and psalms. But Roy and Sally showed me today that all of those things would not make a person a Christian."

A few feet away, Steve Benton moved about nervously. He had heard enough blubbering and confession for one day. It was enough to tear a person apart. Maybe he could wait down the corridor until these people finished their revival service, or maybe he would just tell them that he was going upstairs for a breath of air. But for some reason, he did neither. Instead he stood listening to every emotional word expressed by Nita and Karen.

"How did it happen?" Karen asked, looking first at Sally and Roy and then at Nita. "I thought you told me you were a Christian?"

"I thought I was," Nita admitted. "But when we knew that we were trapped here, I became very much afraid. That's when Sally and Roy said we should say Bible verses that have meant something to us."

"And you couldn't do that?"

"I did not know of any verses that had ever meant something special to me," she confessed. "I had learned many verses in my catechism class, but none of them had special meaning. They were just words."

"When Nita told us this," Sally continued, "I asked her if she had ever personally accepted Jesus Christ as her Saviour. And she had to admit that she didn't ever remember doing that."

Karen looked at Nita in surprise. "But Nita," she said seriously, "You were going to give your testimony at the retreat!"

"I know," she said shaking her head. "And I wonder what I would have said if I had been there to do that."

"I guess God had to let us get stuck down here so we could all get some things taken care of," Roy added.

"Like Nita coming to the Lord," Sally said soberly.

"Yeah," Karen agreed. "And like me getting right with the Lord."

"And it is so wonderful now," Nita finished.

Steve Benton moved closer to the gate.

"And that's why you did all that singing, even while you were trapped?" he asked, not realizing that he had been so personally involved in their conversation.

"Oh, yes," Nita said. "We talked about last week's Sunday school lesson and remembered that Paul and Silas had sung when they were in prison. So we did too."

Steve shook his head slightly as though trying to bring himself out of a trance. He was embarrassed for having entered the conversation.

"And Daddy," Sally said, thrilled that her father had even been listening. "The Bible says that 'all things work together for good to them that love God.' And boy, that sure has been true today."

Steve Benton was visibly relieved when he heard Manchester's bark.

"Hey," he said loudly. "They're back."

As the big German shepherd came running down the corridor, Roy called to him. "Here, Manchester. I have to apologize for calling you 'Fido.'"

The group laughed loudly, relief expressed in every sound.

"Here," Pete said. "I brought a flashlight so we could see what we're doing."

"Good thinking," Steve said. Taking the light, he shined it on Sally. "Here," he said, "let's have a look at your arm first."

107

The others stepped up to look too.

"The scratch isn't deep, but it is bruised," Bob said.

"Yeah, just looks like a bad bruise," Pete agreed.

"Well, I still want you to go to the hospital for a check," Steve said.

"Oh, Dad, it's not that bad," Sally confessed. She had almost forgotten about the pain she had experienced. The thrill of listening to Nita's and Karen's conversation had made her forget all about herself.

Pete Chandler opened his small tool box and began to take out the items they would be using. As he did, Bob Tyler spoke.

"Say, would you kids like to hear what happened at camp today?"

"Sure would," said Roy. "Especially since I was supposed to be in charge of all the arrangements over there."

"Well, let me tell you, someone else took charge—the Lord. Pastor Don just told me that they spent the whole afternoon in prayer," Bob said.

Steve kept working, hoping everyone would think he was not interested in the details of the Bible camp happenings. But Bob Tyler went right on.

"Pastor Don said that they have had the most exciting revival they've ever experienced at camp. Kids are getting straightened out in their Christian lives, and one boy even came to know the Lord as Saviour. Isn't that great?"

Steve grabbed one of the tools and began working feverishly on the gate hinges.

"Almost as great as the things that happened down here today," Roy said happily. "This has to be one of the greatest days in my life."

Karen watched her dad and the others work, trying to release the trapped prisoners.

"Yes, Daddy, wait until you hear what happened down here."

Bob Tyler stopped working and gave his full attention to the teens behind the gate.

"There has been a big revival at the Army academy too," Nita said, offering her hand to Karen as she had done earlier.

Each girl briefly explained the things that had happened to them personally.

"Praise the Lord," Pete Chandler called out, still working on the hinge.

At that moment, the last screw fell out and the three young people suddenly found themselves free. As though on signal, Manchester began to bark excitedly.

"You're right, Manchester," Roy said warmly. "We've had one great day. And we owe a lot of it to you." He stooped down and embraced the big dog. "Thanks, pal, thanks a lot."

"Well," Pete Chandler said as he began to pack away his tools and equipment. "I've got one question I want to ask you, young man."

"Me?" Roy asked somewhat surprised.

"Yes, sir," Pete laughed. "Are you still going to have your singspiration down here tonight?"

Everyone joined in the laughter and chattered away excitedly.

"No way," Roy said firmly. "In fact, we've already had it. Nita and Sally and I have had our

109

singspiration down here. The rest of the group can have theirs wherever they want it."

Karen smiled broadly as she and Nita walked up the concrete stairs arm in arm. Reaching the outside, she stopped and looked back. This would have been a wonderful place for a singspiration, she thought. But she would always remember it as a place of revival. What a wonderful day this had been. She had come back to the Lord, Nita had trusted Jesus Christ as her personal Saviour, and even Sally's dad had heard the gospel about as clearly as it had ever been told. What else could anyone want? Unless it could be a change for Sally's mother too.

And if God could work a miracle like He worked today, then surely He could work in the heart of Sally's mother.